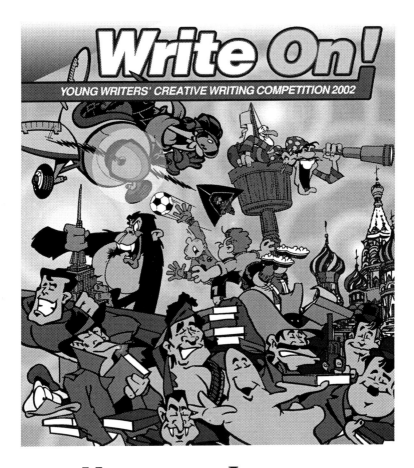

NORTHERN IRELAND

Edited by Steve Twelvetree

First published in Great Britain in 2002 by
YOUNG WRITERS
Remus House,
Coltsfoot Drive,
Peterborough, PE2 9JX
Telephone (01733) 890066

HB ISBN 0 75433 960 2
SB ISBN 0 75433 961 0

FOREWORD

This year, Young Writers proudly presents a showcase of the best short stories and creative writing from today's up-and-coming writers.

We set the challenge of writing for one of our four themes - 'General Short Stories', 'Ghost Stories', 'Tales With A Twist' and 'A Day In The Life Of . . .'. The effort and imagination expressed by each individual writer was more than impressive and made selecting entries an enjoyable, yet demanding, task.

Write On! Northern Ireland is a collection that we feel you are sure to enjoy - featuring the very best young authors of the future. Their hard work and enthusiasm clearly shines within these pages, highlighting the achievement each story represents.

We hope you are as pleased with the final selection as we are and that you will continue to enjoy this special collection for many years to come.

CONTENTS

The Stories

A PIECE OF CAKE

It was a quiet day in Broomhill and a new family, the McKibben's were about to move into number forty-seven. It was a small village and everyone wanted to make friends with them. They did not know this would be a very big mistake.

Peter McKibben went to school the next day and soon made lots of friends. He invited one of them to his house, his name was Christian. Everything was going well until it came to dinner time. Christian asked what was for dinner. Peter was silent until they got to the kitchen. He turned round, Peter was no longer friendly. He looked like he had turned into a madman or he was hypnotised. Christian ran, he ran as fast as he could. Eta, Peter's mum, looked the same and so did his dad. It was like they had turned into zombies. He tried to run but he could not get away. Peter ripped his brain out and put it in a pot. He did the same with his eyes and heart and made them into a cake. The McKibben's started to snigger evilly.

They went around to Christian's house. Then they offered his family the cake. 'Where's Christian?' asked his mother.
'You just ate him,' laughed Eta.
Christian's mother burst into tears and his father tried to phone the police but before he could they turned into mad people and disappeared.

Stephen Wong (11)
All Children's Integrated Primary School, Co Down

THE HOLLOW CARPENTER

A boy of about ten or eleven opened the door of his dad's new Audi. Not waiting for the car to stop he leapt out with a skateboard in one hand. He looked around, his brown spiky hair blocking the sun. He looked around at his new Edwardian style cul-de-sac. He looked down to an older house with an overgrown garden and a *For Sale* sign that looked hundreds of years old. He got on his board. He heard other children his age. One of the kids came up to greet him. 'So lookin' around?' asked the stranger.

'Yeah, my name's Jack, I've just moved in round the top.'

For the next month Jack made new friends but the first person he had met became his best friend. His name was James and as soon as he found out about Jack being good at telling ghost stories, James begged for more. Jack learnt about the old house, that a ghost lived there. He was a carpenter and lived with his wife, but one day a young boy took one of the knives and tripped and stabbed the wife who was bringing him strawberry ice cream. The boy was never found again and this is proof that was shown to Jack by James.

'Wow, what was his name?' asked Jack.

'Sssshhhh, it's not over yet!'

'Sorry.'

'And ever since, the ghost has haunted boys named Jack.'

'Why?'

'Because the boy's name was Jack Lyon.'

Jack's heart missed a beat. Then James said, 'I've gotta go home,' and with that gave Jack an invitation to a Daredevil and Jackass sleepover on Friday from 6pm until Saturday at noon.

Jack went to the party and he was double-black dared to spend a night in the hollow carpenter's house. James grinned. His bony face looked eerie under the greasy hair and darkness.

Jack opened the door, took out his torch and looked around. He walked into what was the drape-covered lounge. He heard the door shut and lock, he set up a small bed and left a paraffin lamp there. Jack went to explore, the floorboards creaked and dead spiders fell from their disintegrated webs. Jack was now approaching the first floor. *Creeeaak.*

Jack looked around in time to see . . . a rather plump mouse squeeze through a rusty door. Jack walked on along the balcony, over the hall then, 'Aaargh!' cough, 'what the?' Jack looked round and saw a familiar face. 'What are you doing here and how come I didn't hear you?' He shook his friend's shoulder who then fell limply off the balcony and landed with a thud. Jack ran down, looked at his friend, then realised there was blood on his hand. A drop of blood landed near Jack. He looked up to see a white person disappear. Jack ran to the door, it was *locked.*

The hollow carpenter strikes again!

The autopsy revealed that James S Murphy had his organs disembowelled and left in a bathtub. Jack M Lyon suffered the same fate.

Jack Lyon (11)
All Children's Integrated Primary School, Co Down

THE KEY

It was a quiet, silent star stricken night in Holland, the year was nineteen thirty-one. A local man called Wilheim was taking a walk with his Jack Russell terrier called Spud. The waves made the only noise as the full moon shone on them. The man started to hear whispers. He cried out, 'I obey him, I obey him!' Finally he fell over and the waves crept around him, and he drowned.

The next day the police were on the scene of the death. Little did they know, he was dead. They thought he had just got lost or ran away because there was no sign of a body or anything else. All there was was the little dog barking endlessly.

The police were confused and left the site to look further along the coast. It was a very windy day, the sun shone brightly and the sand whirled back and forward. A fat, short little man from Germany came to the death site and had a look around. He was a detective and had studied superstitions very much indeed. He saw a black object sticking in the sand, he put a pair of white gloves on and found a piece of metal with three large teeth marks taken out of it. Hans probably was puzzled but said, 'It resembles a half of something and I must find the other half!' He put the piece into his silk handkerchief and put it in his pocket. Hans walked on pretending he hadn't found anything.

He decided to pay a trip to Ireland to examine all the different plant life. Over there a similar incident had happened. It was along a river. A man had said, 'Sandstone,' and then fallen into the mud and drowned in the peat bog next to the river. His wife had said he shouted this before he had drowned as she was walking next to him. She was put in jail for the murder of her husband, Mr Jhonson-White. Hans talked to her even though he struggled to speak English.
Mrs Jhonson-White mumbled, 'I didn't kill him! He tripped and fell into the peat, I tell you!'
Hans believed her.

He travelled back to Holland bearing this in mind. He went back to the murder site. He heard a call as he was walking up the stairs to his flat. It was his secretary calling to him saying, 'Welcome back Sir, there is a parcel for you.' Hans opened it to find another piece exactly the same as the piece he had found before! He joined them together and heard a voice which called out, 'Come! Come!'

Hans fainted. He woke up half an hour later. His secretary looked worried as she thought Hans was dead. He read the note that had come with the other piece of metal. It said:

Dear Hans,

We found where Mr Jhonson-White drowned, there was no body just this piece of metal. We thought it might help you in your investigations.

From,

Irish Police.

Hans stood up and spoke, 'We must go to Egypt.' Hans secretary reluctantly accepted. They went in Han's Ford Tin Lissie (model T) and left Amsterdam and headed for the boat to Egypt. It was a bumpy crossing and it took several weeks to get there.

They asked a local to recommend a hotel, he had a pale face and bloodshot eyes and said, 'Come, come!' like the voice he had heard before. They followed the Egyptian up the sandstone stairs to a huge area full of olden day workers, but it was a secret! It was as if he was in Ancient Egypt! He recognised some of the workers as they passed by, they were Mr Jhonson-White and Wilheim! There had been many murders along the coast recently and when they died they must have come here to work! He looked down to his feet, then upwards to find he was an Egyptian king or was dressed as one anyway. His secretary was a maid standing next to him. He tried to speak but he could only speak in Ancient Egyptian.

A funny thing was that one day in our time was forty in theirs. Hans decided to build new pyramids and new homes for the people, so roughly every week a new pyramid arose. This puzzled hundreds of people and only Hans knew how.

Today Hans wishes to come back to this time but little does he know that seventy-two years have passed! In case you are wondering what the two black objects were that Hans found, they made a key which put him in the past. Hans will have to find the white key to get to the present.

Wills McNeilly (11)
All Children's Integrated Primary School, Co Down

THE SCARY GHOST

One time I went to an estate and I saw a house torn apart, it was dusty and creepy on the outside. I decided to go and see what was inside, so I scuttled along and discovered what was in the house. When I got to the rusty door I noticed the hinges of the door handle were coming off so I thought I would push the door gently. After I pushed the door open I saw that there were stairs leading up to a little hallway, I began to wander up the stairs. On my way up I noticed pictures of all the famous artists, for example Vincent Van Gogh. I went down the hallway and I felt a little breeze behind my back, it felt like a fan and when I turned round there was nothing there. I got frightened a little bit but I went on very quickly and tried to find out what had happened.

I saw a shadow when I turned my head around, it was getting bigger and bigger. I thought it was a person trying to murder me. It was nothing like a person. I began to hear, 'Whooo! Whooo' in my ear and then the sound stopped and I heard nothing at all until, 'Booo!' I jumped and saw a ghost. I screamed for help until I noticed it was my sister Mandy under a white sheet.

Shane Rush (11)
All Children's Integrated Primary School, Co Down

THE HOUSE OF EVIL

One day a woman called Mary gave birth to twins, they were both girls. She was a single parent. Two days later she decided to call one of them Laura and one of them Anna. Laura was born ten seconds before Anna. All the strength went into Laura and all of the scrap that was left went into Anna.

Since Laura was so smart she started school when she was three years old. Years flew by and when they were nine years old Mary decided to move away for a while to France. They moved into a deep, dark, gloomy house that had been haunted for centuries.

As they walked through the door all they could see were long spiderwebs hanging above the door. There was a crack on the roof leading up the stairs. Mary and the twins walked quietly up the stairs and into the bathroom. They looked in the toilet and found a head as white as a sheet with one eye floating in the water, blood splashing out of its neck. It also had teeth sticking out of its nose. Laura turned around to find the rest of its body lying in the bath. She only noticed that one of its legs was chopped off and one arm sliced off and stuck to the handle of the door, also four of its fingers were stuck to the taps of the sink.

Mary was shocked, scared and horrified all at the same time and suddenly they heard a creak in the bedroom. Mary went in and found three black kittens nibbling at chicken and drinking some milk. She took them outside so they could run wild in the field. When Mary came back in she found a note saying . . .

'Beware of this house
It's not the best
But it will do until you die and rest'.

Mary ran upstairs to find that Laura and Anna were tied up. She untied them and tried to find who it was but there was no one in sight. Then she noticed that there was a man in his mid-fifties, perhaps he was the owner of the house before them, he was called Paddy Grant.

They climbed out of the window and jumped into their BMW to find that their back window was smashed to pieces. They went to the police station and told them the whole story of what had happened. The police went and searched the house from top to bottom but found no one alive, but they did find four dead kittens and two cats, three mice dead and cut open and one man in the bathroom who was covered in blood.

Mary, Laura and Anna moved back to where they used to live and that was in England.

Mary got married again and had more children and lived in a big, lovely cottage.

Leanne Mills (11)
All Children's Integrated Primary School, Co Down

GONE IN ONE NIGHT!

One dark night in January two boys were playing football. When John kicked the football into a dark, grey house David said, 'That's my best ball. I'm getting it back.' They walked through the tall doorway. 'You go that way, I'll go this way,' David groaned. David walked into an empty living room, he tripped over a brick and hit his head on a bookcase.

John was looking frantically for David, then he found him lying on the floor. 'Are you alright?' John yelped.
'Yes, I fell over a brick. Hey, look at that it's a slide,' David shouted.
'Let's go down it,' John said.
'Yuck, smells of rotten fish,' exclaimed David.
'No, it's a dead man, let's get out of here,' John yelled.
He was hung by his nose, only had one eye, one arm and one leg.
'Run for the window,' David screamed.

When they got out they bumped into a tall man with deep ringed eyes. They ran into an underground tunnel. People say that they were shot and others say that the tunnel caved in on them. Three days later the police gave up because they couldn't find the two boys anywhere, so the police treated themselves to a doughnut and some coffee.

Four years later

The two boys, John and David were found yesterday. They were found beside another man. They were hung by their noses and had six swords in each of them. A man in his forties has been jailed for life. The boys were trailed into the house and their mouths were stitched closed.

Gerard McConkey (11)
All Children's Integrated Primary School, Co Down

THE ALIEN THAT CAME FOR TEA

One day I looked out of my window and I saw a flying saucer. Then the doorbell rang, I opened the door slowly and there on the front doorstep stood an alien. He said, 'Bla, bla, bla, bla, bla, bla, bla,' and then he started to fiddle with his watch, and he started to talk like me. He said, 'I am very hungry, can I stay for tea?'

'Oh yes, I would love that,' I said, so we had ice cream and jelly, cake, sandwiches and sweets.

He ate some ice cream and it came out of his nose. He ate some jelly and he wobbled for two hours, and then he ate some salad and his eyes turned into tomatoes. Then he had some juice and his arms started leaking and he started to sprinkle juice over the flowers. I laughed and laughed. I had a great time with Mr Alien, but then I woke up.

Joanna Wilson (8)
Annaghmore Primary School, Co Armagh

THE SHOOTING MAN

Once there was a man who was shooting in a field, he was shooting crows, pigeons and other birds. He shot all sorts of birds. He shot ten crows and twenty pigeons.

One day he thought he was in trouble. The owner of the field could see him shooting in his field so the farmer came up to him and said, 'Hello there.'
He replied, 'Hello there.'
The owner of the field said, 'I'm glad you're shooting these birds because they were eating away at this year's crop. When we weren't there they just ate and ate, so that's why I'm glad you are shooting them. All the farmers around the country need you because they are having awful trouble with the birds too.'

So the farmers all had good crops the next year!

Kane Douglas (8)
Annaghmore Primary School, Co Armagh

THE FOOTBALLER

There is a footballer called Owen, he plays for Liverpool. The manager called Gerard Houllier said that they were going to play against Madrid. Everybody gasped because Madrid had some world class players!

So the night of the big match came. Both teams came out onto the pitch. Madrid won the kick-off. Riise got the ball, he kicked it up the field to Gerrard. Gerrard passed it to Heskey, Heskey to Owen and Owen whacked it between the goalposts. The half-time oranges tasted even more juicy now!

It was 1-0 at half-time. Liverpool had definitely had more of the ball, look at the magnificent goal Owen had scored. The goalie never had a chance!

It's Liverpool's kick-off and Owen passed it to Heskey, Heskey passed it to Owen and Owen scored again. Now it's 2-0. Madrid were getting whipped! It's one minute to full time and then suddenly the game was over. Liverpool had won the Cup. The manager, the team and their fans celebrated all night!

Stephen Farrell (8)
Annaghmore Primary School, Co Armagh

THE GHOST

It all started when I was going to my friend Tim's house. When I got there I went in and Tim said, 'Do you want to play hide-and-seek?'
'Yes I do,' I said. So we played hide-and-seek. I was counting and I looked everywhere and when I looked in his house I finally found him.

I wasn't happy because Tim had stopped playing and he hadn't bothered to tell me. I couldn't understand it. 'I thought we were playing hide-and-seek,' I said.
'No we weren't,' Tim said.
'I'm going,' I said.
'I'll get your shoes,' Tim said.
'I can get them myself,' I said.
'No you won't,' said Tim.
'Just watch me,' I said.

So I went to get my shoes, but as I went to walk away from the house I saw something hanging Tim's mum up on the roof.
The ghost said, 'Just hang her there.'

Then I ran home and said, 'Mum, something has killed Tim's mum.'
'Oh dear, I'll go and ring the police,' said Mum.
But it was too late. The ghost just blew the phone up and it got a gun.
I had an idea. I phoned the police on my mobile phone. 'Hurry up. Mum it's coming. Hurry, it's coming into the house.'

The police arrived and shot their guns into the air. They scared the ghost so much that it never came back.

Ashley Runnett (8)
Annaghmore Primary School, Co Armagh

FAT CAT ALFIE IN LOVE

One day Fat Alfie and Charlie the wimp were watching something most beautiful. Something that smelt so sweet, it was Honey. Honey was the cat that lived next door. Honey didn't like Alfie but Alfie liked her.

Charlie came from the junkyard, she was a junkyard cat and she smelt revolting. 'Poo,' said Honey, 'you are so disgusting hanging around with this jerk!'
'Yuck!' she repeated, 'I am out of here.'
'Fine,' said Alfie, 'I hate you.'
Honey's heart sank into a deep sorrow, she was so sad that she ran up a tree and cried.

Next day Alfie and Honey got married and then the two of them and Charlie went to the beach. Luckily Charlie smelt of sea water today! They went to look for seashells on the shore.

Then they went to the swimming pool, Honey showed off doing somersaults in the water.

After that the two of them went through the 'Tunnel of Love', and then they watched the sun go down and fade away, together.

Rebekah-Lee Ferguson (8)
Annaghmore Primary School, Co Armagh

THE FOX AND THE GOOSE

Once upon a time there was a fox. The fox loved to go to the farmyards, but there was one farm in particular that he liked to visit. He liked to eat geese. He did this so often, that the police were offering a £10,000 reward to the one who could catch the fox who loved to eat the geese.

One day the fox was out hunting for geese but instead he found a horse. The horse was eating peacefully until the fox came. The fox tried to get past the horse, but the horse did not let him past. Quickly the horse kicked him and the farmer was amazed that the fox was not dead.

The policemen caught the fox and took him to the Wildlife Park and the police found the horse a new field.

Dalton Ashfield Beattie (8)
Annaghmore Primary School, Co Armagh

THE POWERFUL UNICORN

Once long, long ago there was a unicorn who lived happily on her own. But one day while she was eating her fresh grass she heard something loud and ran towards it. When she got close she had to stop and have a wee peep at what the noise was. When she looked through the long grass all she could see was a unicorn running away from something.

Then she saw it, it was a man with a gun trying to kill the other unicorn. Then he saw her but she took to her heels and ran towards the other unicorn.

Just then she heard another noise, the man with the gun was cutting down trees to get a better view of the unicorns. He wanted to try and kill them to make money.

The male unicorn went up behind the man and called for the lady unicorn to come over too, and she did. He told her to use her magical power on him and she did. It blew him into space and they lived happily ever after.

Chloe Collins (9)
Annaghmore Primary School, Co Armagh

DUCHESS THE HORSE

There was a girl called Joanna. She was eleven years old. She lived at number twenty-eight Meadow Lane in the country. She loved the countryside.

When she goes to school she sees a black mare every day. She wondered who owned that beautiful horse. Ever since she was little she had wanted a horse. She knew this was the one she loved.

So every day she would go out and work. She would feed her neighbour's chickens and geese and each day her piggy bank got heavier. One day her piggy bank was so heavy she couldn't lift it!

She did this all just to get a horse, it wasn't just any horse she wanted, she loved the black mare.

One day she found the horse's owner and she asked him if she could buy it, and the man said yes. She was so happy she couldn't sleep that night.

So one day when she had enough money saved up, her dad went with her to pay the man and they bought the mare home.

She called her Duchess. Every day Joanna would brush Duchess' mane until the sun would go down. Joanna's love still shows today for Duchess.

Jodie Richardson (8)
Annaghmore Primary School, Co Armagh

A BIRTHDAY SURPRISE

In a village called Smallville there were seven children called David, Bob, Jill, Kane, Alison, Peter and Christine. They were all best friends. Every day after school they took turns going to each other's houses.

On Monday they went to Alison's. Tuesday they went to Bob's. Wednesday they all went to Christine's. Thursday then went to David's. Friday they went to Jill's. Saturday they went to Kane's and they went to Peter's on Sunday.

It was a Tuesday and they were at Bob's. Bob liked building things. Every time they went to one of the boy's houses the girls brought teddies and they watched television, while the boys played football and built with Lego.

It came to the fifth of May, it was one month and twenty-six days to Peter's birthday. David, Bob, Jill, Kane, Alison and Christine were not at school they were buying balloons, party hats, party things and lots more. Peter was sitting at home.

Peter's friends were whispering behind his back. Peter did not know what he had done to upset his friends. When school was over Peter's friends left early for the party.

When Peter got home everybody was there. There were balloons, party hats, birthday cake and lots of food. Peter said it was the happiest day of his life.

Richard Martin (9)
Annaghmore Primary School, Co Armagh

ACE COMBAT

The year is two thousand and forty. First the cannon Alpha Prime was used to shoot down the falling stars, but when the stars stopped falling the cannon began a war. It was used to fight and wage war instead of defending Earth.

One bright summer morning, I was cycling to school when I saw two aeroplanes dog fighting in the sky. I couldn't tear my gaze away from them. Suddenly one of the planes shot down the other. It fell in a cove, the cove that my family lived in. I looked up at the victor, there was the number six emblazoned in yellow.

Now I'm twenty years old, I am a pilot still searching for the Russian Mig that killed my family.
'Private Campbell!' roared General Grim. 'Wakey, wakey!'
I jumped up. Quickly I put on my uniform. Today was the day some other ace pilots and I were to escort a bombing squadron to a Russian hanger which is based in Kentucky.

I got into my Raptor plane and left our airfield hanger far behind. 'Okay people,' echoed Private Bob Wills in my ear, 'remember what we came for.'
'Yeah we know, escort the bomber boys and come home,' said Will, my younger brother.
'And throw a party!' shouted Jack, our party animal.
Suddenly out of nowhere came four Russian Migs.
'Take them down!' I shouted. I went zooming after the leader.
'You're mine, rookie!' he said.
'Not today I think,' I replied calmly. This really got him mad. He chased after me spraying machine-gun fire everywhere. I got a lock on him and fired two missiles at him. 'Yeah!' I shouted wildly. We had taken them all down, but victory came at a price. My brother ended up with a broken neck.

Two years later and General Grim has informed us that he has been told by the President of the United States that this is to be our last assignment. We are all going on a raid on the Russians biggest headquarters in the United States.

When we saw our target looming in the distance I saw my hated nemesis.

'Let's dance rookie,' he taunted. I fired my machine-guns at him. He returned fire freely. 'Too bad I have to kill such a good pilot!' he said. Then I let loose two missiles and blew him out of the sky.

Peter Conan (8)
Annaghmore Primary School, Co Armagh

MY FAVOURITE POP GROUP

I have loved S Club 7 ever since I was five and I have always wanted to see them. Mummy went to work and got out at lunchtime and she tried to get three tickets for Joanna, herself and me to see S Club 7. They were ten pounds per ticket. She rang me at Valerie's house and told me she *had* got tickets for S Club 7 and that they were for 24th October, 2003. Today was the 3rd May, 2002. I had to wait more than a year. I marked down the date carefully on the calendar. I hated waiting but at least we had the tickets!

At last it was October. After school each day I raced home to mark off the calendar. The third came, the tenth came and soon it was the twenty-fourth. It was the day to see S Club 7. I barged into Mummy and Daddy's room, 'Today is the day!' I said.

We had bought lots of sweets to bring with us. We put on our clothes and I could hardly eat my breakfast I was so excited. We went to pick up Joanna and then started the car journey to the Odyssey, in Belfast, where the concert was. This seemed to take forever.

We screamed, when at last, our favourite band came out on stage. They started the show with the song, 'Never Had A Dream Come True' and then they sang my favourite, 'Reach'.

They talked to the audience and asked people to come up, Joanna and I waved our hands in the air. We were chosen. We couldn't believe it! We had a brilliant time.

Rachel Clarke (8)
Annaghmore Primary School, Co Armagh

THE HAUNTED SCHOOL OF BALLYBEEN

One day a detective looked at the newspaper and it said, 'Murder at Ballybeen school'.

When the detective went to check it out there was blood all around the haunted school. He wanted to know more so he asked people about it. Someone said the ghost of the school was called Peeves and he died during the fire of Ballybeen, that he was rich and that he guards his gold from everyone and will kill anyone who gets in his way.

As the weeks went by more murders occurred. One night he went to check it out. When he got to the door it opened by itself and he walked in. He heard a ghostly voice saying, 'Who dares to disturb me? Leave the school now!'
The detective heard the voice coming from upstairs. When he ran up to check it out he saw something behind the curtains.

When he went to check it out fire blasted around the curtains. A clown ghost flew out the window and its eyes turned into fire. A man came in and turned the lights on. Then the ghost went into his body and when he woke up he was in hospital beside the detective. The man thanked him but when he went away his eyes glowed like fire . . .

Kyle Davidson (10)
Brooklands Primary School, Co Antrim

MY AMAZING ADVENTURE

Suddenly I was falling very fast! Everything was going as dark as the night sky and I was crushed with lots of others like me. If I was going to be here a while I was going to sleep.

I was awoken by the door opening and a bright light. I thought I would escape, but a chubby man was lifting me and putting me in a sack and then he threw me in the back of a van.

We were off at a great speed. We stopped. I was lifted out of the sack with the others and we were sorted into groups, then put back into the dreaded sack. Next we were madly thrown into something that sounded very loud. How would we ever escape?

Roughly about eighteen hours later, with no fresh air, we were lifted into another van, it zoomed away. Suddenly we came to a halt and the sack was opened. Would this be our chance to escape? It seemed different here because it was so hot and sunny.

The man lifted me out and squeezed me through a miniature hole. A young girl ran excitedly towards me and shouted, 'Mum, my birthday card's here from granny in England!

Sherry Morrow (10)
Brooklands Primary School, Co Antrim

MY FIRST TRAINING

One day I called my father and asked if I could have my first hunting lessons with him. He told me to get some sticks and bits of flint. He sharpened the stick and tied some string to another stick, put feathers on the sharpened stick and that made a bow and arrow. Then he got a longer stick and sharpened it. That made a spear. He did the same for me, only making smaller ones.

Then off we went to the forest and saw a plump pig and deer. He told me to keep my balance, not to rush, take my time, aim and let go. I did exactly that and missed the target. I looked at my father, he wasn't there. Then I heard a roar and turned round. I saw my father kill the deer. That's how you kill close up. He then told me how to throw a spear and kill it. I tried it and threw a spear that killed a boar. We took it home and ate it for supper.

We went hunting again the next day and I killed a pheasant with a bow and arrow.
'I love hunting,' I told him. I loved it.

David Hume (10)
Brooklands Primary School, Co Antrim

ATTACK OF THE WITCH

One dark, cold night a boy called Oliver and a girl called Maggie decided to go on a walk through the graveyard.

'I want to go home,' said Maggie frightfully.

'Oh, don't be a baby,' Oliver said bravely.

'Wh-wh-what was that?' Maggie whispered.

'I don't know,' Oliver said.

'It's a witch!' they screamed.

They ran home as quickly as their legs could carry them. 'She is getting closer, hurry,' Maggie cried out. Oliver rushed to open the door, but it was stuck. They ran to the back door, it was open. When they got in they locked the door behind them and sprinted to the bedroom. As soon as they got to the bedroom they slammed the door shut. All they heard was a *tap, tap, tap*. Every minute they heard a single footstep. Then they heard their door knob rattling. 'She's getting closer!' Maggie cried. 'OK, OK, find the nearest window and we will see if we can all climb out of it.'

The door slowly began to open. Suddenly they opened their eyes, then they said, 'We imagined it all?'

Asta Hewitt (10)
Brooklands Primary School, Co Antrim

A DAY IN THE LIFE OF DAVID BECKHAM

It's 7.30am and David Beckham's day is just about to start. His alarm clock goes off in his hotel room, which is in the middle of Japan. Today is the 30th June 2002, the World Cup Final. He gets up, he cleans his teeth and gets washed. He eats his bowl of Frosties and waits for the bus to collect the team. At 11.30am Victoria rings him on his mobile to say good luck and to score a free kick for their son Brooklyn.

Soon the whole England team are on the bus and on their way to the World Cup Final. They will see hundreds of fans on the way to the ground and they all start to get very nervous, everyone except David Beckham. He knows that they will win and that he will score that free kick for his son. They get off the bus and start their training.

3.00pm comes and he leads the team out onto the pitch to play Brazil in the World Cup Final, with millions watching all over the world.

Ronaldo scores first for Brazil. Then Beckham crosses for Heskey to score a header at the back post. With five minutes to go, Owen is fouled outside the box. The world watches as David steps up to take the free kick. He shoots, he scores! England are the world champions and it's all thanks to David Beckham.

He winks at the camera, at his son and he kisses the badge on his shirt, it's another day in the life of David Beckham.

Gary Davidson (10)
Brooklands Primary School, Co Antrim

A Day In The Life Of A Bee

I woke up to the sound of all the bees buzzing around in the hive. I flew away in search of nectar. Suddenly something caught my eye - bright red petals. Like a greedy child wanting sweets, I dived into the flower and then into another until I had satisfied my hunger. With my tummy bulging, it was time to return to the hive and do some work.

To my horror when I arrived back, there was a big van with the words *Bee Exterminator* - I alerted the queen bee, who immediately ordered me to round up the army and take them to her.

The queen bee informed everyone about the situation and commanded us to hurry to our positions. We stood like soldiers at the entrance to the hive waiting for the enemy to attack. A man in a white suit stepped out, we attacked him immediately with our awful stings. I crawled in under his mask and stung his nose. He swiped me away and dashed back to his van and drove away. The queen bee awarded me for my quick thinking. What a brilliant day!

Lisa Armour (10)
Fairview Primary School, Co Antrim

A Day In The Life Of A Butterfly

It is cold and dark in my cocoon. I can't see anything. Wait! There's a speck of light appearing. It's time to break free. Here I come into the big wide world. Look, I'm a beautiful butterfly! I'll lie in the sun and dry my wings.

Now it's time to fly. Oh no, I'm dropping to the ground. Phew! I'm up in the air again. Flying is great fun, up and down and round and round.

A window is open, I'll fly in and see the house. There's a lovely plant in the hall. Ouch! It's very prickly. As I fly away I become stuck in a cobweb. The spider's coming towards me. Help! A human rushes to save me, she knocks down the web and sets me free.

Into the garden I fly and search for a leaf to eat for tea. Yum, yum, that was delicious. I enjoy myself, flitting from flower to flower.

Evening is drawing near and I'm getting very tired. I'll find somewhere to sleep for the night. There's a great big leaf over in the corner. I'll shelter there at the end of a happy day.

Sarah-Jane Montgomery (10)
Fairview Primary School, Co Antrim

A Day In The Life Of David Beckham

I was ready for the World Cup Final but Victoria had different plans, she insisted I go shopping . . . again! How could I refuse?

As soon as we stepped out of the car we were mobbed by photographers and football fans, wanting autographs. Brooklyn can't even write yet but he obliged with slobbery kisses instead.

When we finally reached Victoria's favourite shop, she ordered Brooklyn and I to wait at the hairdressing salon whilst she chose new accessories for her best dress. I glanced into the salon and saw a boy having yellow tips put in his hair. I fancied them and paid the hairdresser to do mine. When Victoria arrived she was *not* pleased.

Again we pushed our way through the autograph hunters and eventually reached the car. We crawled along the motorway as it was now the rush hour and we reached the stadium as *the final whistle blew.*

Angrily I swung the car round and headed for home as fast as I could. I switched on the television just in time to hear the commentator say 'If only David Beckham had been in the squad, England might have won!'

I climbed upstairs to bed. This was the worst day of my life.

Matthew Barr (10)
Fairview Primary School, Co Antrim

SPOOKMANIA

Once upon a hot summer's day, I boarded a plane to an island in the middle of the ocean, the seven seas. I parachuted down and when I got there, I explored.

I woke up one morning and saw a sad-looking ghost, it freaked me out at first, then I found out its name was Ghosty. The more we saw of each other, the more friendly we got (I saw a lot of him).

I woke the next morning and heard shooting. The animals were in danger! I got there in time. A gang of poachers were just about to shoot a wild boar (for food as meat).

Ghosty scared one of the poachers away, then he scared two more away and then he scared four more away. Ghosty scared eight more away and then he scared the last one. I went to get the plane back home, I hugged Ghosty as tight as I could hug him and when I got home I told my mum, it was a long story.
She said 'Go again next year then - won't you?'

Alex Scott (8)
Fairview Primary School, Co Antrim

MY FREAKY NIGHT

One Hallowe'en night I, Francine Butterworth, was having a party in a mansion, a *really spooky* mansion which had not been used for over a thousand years.

It all happened when I went upstairs, because I was bursting for the loo, after too much punch. I was about to open the door when I heard a creepy noise and then I heard *'Whoo!Whoo!'* I was *really* freaked out.

I tried to open the door but it was locked and I heard again *'Whoo! Whoo!'* I saw a white hand come out of the door. After about two hours, I finally met the thing, it was a *ghost!*

He introduced himself and his name was George the ghost. So we went downstairs and met everyone and we partied from 7.00pm - 2.00am.
I still go to his house in Ghost city.

Sophie Heaton (8)
Fairview Primary School, Co Antrim

COUSIN CRISIS

On the 13th January, Sharon and I had a spooky encounter. So will I tell you? Okay . . .

I was coming home from school (finally) when I saw this spooky mansion. No one had lived in it for thousands of years and I wanted to check it out, so I went in. *Big mistake!*

As soon as I went in I saw a pair of red glowing eyes. I tried to run but my legs were stiff. Then it emerged . . . a funny looking *ghost!* We introduced ourselves. He told me his name was Boo! Then he told me what was happening.

He said he had some bad relatives and they were haunting number 13, which was my house, so we had to get them out.

As soon as I went into my house there was a *'Whoo! Whoo!'* They were in my house alright. I had to get them out. But how? I thought for about an hour and then I got it. If we pretended we were not scared, they would get bored and go away. So we did this and they went away!

I kept visiting Boo and we lived *scarily* ever after!

Emma Reid (8)
Fairview Primary School, Co Antrim

A DAY IN THE LIFE OF A BEE

'Buzz!' Came the alarm from the chief worker bee. I opened my eyes and yawned. I stretched my wings and fluttered over to the breakfast table to eat my delicious home-made honey nut flakes. I looked at the time, 7 o'clock, I'm late!

I flew to my Bzz 2000 and sped off down the road, past some jealous girls and furious boys. I sped into the car park and paid the parking ticket in Bzzetas. I flew into the entrance and set my eyes upon the horrors that I would face today. The Queen Bee's Surprise Inspection!

I froze with my leg in my pockets. The queen bee was flying along a red carpet, shaking antennae. I fluttered to the end of the line as if I was being chased by a fly swatter. Moments later the queen flew in front of me. 'What's your name, young man?' She asked.
'Paul O'Nate, Ma'am,' I said.
'Pleasure meeting you Paul,' the queen bee said. With one final wave to the buzzing crowd, the queen bee flew back to Buckingham Beehive.

What a stressful day this has been for me, I'm glad it's over.

Mark Sewell (9)
Fairview Primary School, Co Antrim

A DAY IN THE LIFE OF GARY LONGWELL

At the start of the day, Gary Longwell would get up at six o'clock. He would get his training gear, including two pairs of tracksuit bottoms, three thick jumpers, one tracksuit (winter training gear) and a pair of shorts, two light T-shirts, two pairs of socks (summer training gear) gum shield, scrum hat and a head band (all year round training gear).

After he gets dressed, he drives to Ulster Rugby Club and meets up with the team at about eight o'clock. They start training, first they run around the rugby field about four times, then they start running in a defence line, passing the ball. Then they get the tackling bags out and by this time, the day is over.

They go and then start another day.

Christopher Millar (8)
Fairview Primary School, Co Antrim

A Day In the Life Of Jeremy McWilliams

One morning, Jeremy McWilliams was just out of bed when he asked his wife to fill his motorbike with petrol for the World Superbike race. So off she went down to the garage to put some petrol into his bike. She accidentally put in some Coke instead. She did this because Jeremy had taken off the Coke label, so it looked like petrol.

Jeremy had his breakfast and got ready to go. He started his motorbike and off he went. He got halfway to the race, when he went *Wah! And fell off!*

When he tried to go, the bike wouldn't start. He saw a petrol station sign saying, *half a mile to the petrol station*, so he walked there, pushing his bike. When he got there he filled the bike and remembered that the race was tomorrow!

Scott Barr (8)
Fairview Primary School, Co Antrim

A RIDE ON THE GHOST TRAIN

One night, Emily, Jessica and I went to Barry's in Portrush. We went on the ghost train. It was quite scary because we just sat on a carriage and went round. On the way round, there was a skeleton and he jumped up at us.

After it was over, we went to get some chips and then we had to go home. When we got home, we had to go to bed because it was nearly one o'clock in the morning. But Emily said to her mum, 'I am *not* going to bed!'
Mummy said 'Oh yes you are!'
'No I am not. All right then, but can I go back to Barry's tomorrow?'
'Only if you go to bed now,' said Mummy.

In the morning, again they went to Dreamworld instead of going to Portrush. Nicola, Jessica and Emily went on the balloons in Dreamworld. They also went on the train as well and they really liked it. Their little tag was nearly done so they used it up by going on a few more rides. They went on the train, the slides and the balloons again. After that, they went home happy and tired.

Nicola Lennon (8)
Fairview Primary School, Co Antrim

THE BLUE FALCON

Once upon a time in Yugoslavia a boy called John was asleep. Then a shadow lit up on the wall. As quick as a flash, he was swiped out of his room and out onto the street.

Suddenly he heard a voice saying, 'I am the ghost of the Blue Falcon. I like to kill people. I will take you back to my den. You will die! Ha, ha, ha, ha, ha, ha.'

He took him back to his den and said to him, 'Do you know who I am?' John said 'No, I have not a clue who you are.'
The Blue Falcon said, 'OK the death begins!'
Suddenly a robotic dog blasted through the window. The Blue Falcon fell down an open drain, the dog had pushed him down. The next night John slept peacefully.

Philip Hutchinson (8)
Fairview Primary School, Co Antrim

MAX AND THE GHOST

Last summer Max went out for a walk in the park when he saw a house. He saw something move!

Max said, 'No one lives there.' But he didn't know about the ghost. He went inside it and it looked like the TV movie 'On To The Ghost'! Max went up to the top of the house. When he got to the top he looked down. He saw a light and a door and he went inside but he got lost. He saw a TV and said 'I'm lost but I can watch TV.' Max put the TV on and watched 'My Love'.

Max was lost for six hours. He went up to a room and got stuck for six hours. His whole body was stuck. He yelled 'I'm stuck!'

The ghost came and got Max out. 'Thank you' said Max.
The ghost said 'I'm Ed.'
In an hour, they were best friends.

Max heard a sound, he heard someone yell 'Cut.'
The lights went on 'Hey you, you are on TV.'
Max said 'But I thought this was real,'
'No' said the man.
'This is 'On to the ghost'.'

Healey Blair (8)
Fairview Primary School, Co Antrim

A Day In The Life Of Superman

Once upon a time Superman was standing about with nothing to do except twiddle his thumbs. There were no crimes about. There weren't any bombs in any of the big buildings. He asked lots of people to do bad things but they all said, 'No!' Then he asked one more person and luckily for Superman he said, 'Yes!'

The man planted a big, fizzy, black bomb in the Empire State Building. Superman pretended to everyone that he didn't know about the bomb but he really did. No one else knew about the bomb except him.

He waited for a little while, then he said to Lois Lane, 'There is a bomb in the Empire State Building and I have to get rid of it so that no one gets hurt.'

Superman went to where the bomb was planted. It was a tough job for him to find it and get it out of the building. When he got it out, he threw it with all his strength into outer space where it exploded safely. Thanks to Superman the world was saved again.

Christopher Stanford (8)
Fairview Primary School, Co Antrim

SANTA IN TROUBLE

One day Santa was in a bar having a pint. Then two pints. Then three pints. When he came out, he went into his apartment and went to sleep. Tomorrow was Christmas Eve. The next day he went back to the bar. He had three pints, then that night he couldn't drive the sleigh so he sent a letter to me. The letter said, 'Dear Conor and Aidan, I am too drunk to drive my sleigh so can you do it for me?'

So Aidan and I went to Santa's apartment. He showed us the sleigh. When I saw it, I was amazed. He took us into the stable where he kept the reindeer and showed us Rudolph. When we saw him, we thought what a nose. The clock struck midnight, so Aidan and I tied the reindeer to the sleigh and jumped in. The sleigh started to move and suddenly we were in the air.

We finished Ireland, then we went to England. After that we went to Scotland and then Wales. Then America, after that France, then Spain and Sweden. After that we came home.

Santa thanked us and said 'Well done.' It was very hard work.
Santa said, 'I will never do that again,' and flew back to Lapland.

Conor McKenna (9)
St Anne's Primary School, Belfast, Co Antrim

SCARY

One Hallowe'en night my mum and dad were at a Hallowe'en party and my sister Niamh was babysitting my brother and I. We were eating popcorn and watching Harry Potter. We had seen it before and were getting a bit bored. We all fell asleep.

I heard a knock at the door, I got up to answer it and took my brother's baseball bat. I looked out of the window, there was a man dressed in black. I opened the door and started hitting the person with the baseball bat, when the person turned around, it was my dad dressed in a vampire.

My dad was really tired and went to bed and my mum had just put the cars in the garage because last Hallowe'en boys came round to her new car and threw eggs at it. My mum was really tired too so I kept the baseball bat beside me to be safe.

I heard a knock at the door again. I looked out of the window and got the bat. I opened the door. I thought I knew the person. I asked why was he here. He said, 'I know your mum and dad.'
I asked him to wait outside but he said, 'No.'
I tried to close the door but then he put his arm in the way. I closed the door and his arm was badly bleeding so I brought him into the kitchen. I asked his name. He said, 'I am called John.' I told him to stay in the kitchen while I went to get my mum and dad. When I came back with my dad he had disappeared.

My dad told me I must be seeing things. My dad went out of the room, then I heard a wooing noise. I ran for the kitchen door, it slammed closed. I was so scared, I stayed in the kitchen all night. At last I fell asleep and when I woke up everything was the same.

Aoife Barr (9)
St Anne's Primary School, Belfast, Co Antrim

SANTA'S IN TROUBLE

The day before Christmas Eve Santa fell asleep and the elves went into the woods. A man who was dressed in black stole Santa's magic dust. He had a big black dog who was very fierce.

The next day it was Christmas Eve and Santa couldn't find his elves, so he called his wife and said, 'Honey have you seen my elves?'
She said, 'No, I haven't, why?'
'Because they've got the toys,' Santa said.

So Santa went out in the woods and started looking there and the big dark man hid behind the trees.

The man found the elves wandering about so he tiptoed over and grabbed the elves and he shouted 'Santa I have your elves so come and get them.' Santa rushed over to the man. He said he had to give him a thousand pounds.

Santa ran home and opened his Monopoly game and thought he could put his fake Monopoly game money into a bag and give it to the man and he could run before he realised it was fake money. So that's what he did and he was able to give out the presents after all.

The next day everyone had a lovely Christmas except the man and the dog.

Eadaoin Malone (9)
St Anne's Primary School, Belfast, Co Antrim

One Very Unusual Day

Every day when I go to school, I meet my best friend Eadaoin at my line and Eadaoin and I go and play skips, or else take turns on having a go on her jumping hoop which she got for her birthday, but today that's just not what happened . . .

It was a lovely Monday morning, the sun shining and there wasn't a grey cloud in sight for miles around. Although I hated having to do loads of work and getting tons of homework, I quite liked school because every day when I arrived, I got to see Eadaoin and we would play together, we even had some great handshakes!

Frank, my taxi driver, had just left me off at the layby and I was walking up through the car park to my line to meet Eadaoin, when I thought I felt someone open my bag and take something out. When I swung round to see who was there, no one was there, so I decided to forget about it and I sprinted on up to my line.

There was Eadaoin standing at the line waiting for me but she seemed to be looking for something, so I ran up to her and asked 'Have you lost something?'
She answered 'Well actually someone seems to have stolen my skipping rope and my jumping hoop,'
'Well that's funny,' I said 'because I seem to have also lost my skipping ropes and my new jumping hoop,'
'Well if we want to get back our belongings, we'd better start by checking who has got new stuff,' said Eadaoin very determinedly . . .
but just as we were about to start looking, the bell rang, 'Darn, we'll have to start looking at break' said Eadaoin, and I totally agreed.

All morning we had these awful maths tests and I'm not very good at maths, in fact, I'm rubbish so I didn't really enjoy that morning and I kept on looking at the clock, but time seemed to pass really slowly.

Then the bell rung, me and Eadaoin sprinted out of the door and began our search at once.

We checked every playground but nowhere did we find our lost belongings, but in the forest beside our school, there were loads of bangs and bumps and yippees and that made us suspicious . . .

At lunchtime, I go to dinners and she goes to lunches, so we decided to meet over by the forest and at lunchtime when everyone went out to play, we would go and investigate in the forest to see what or who was making those noises and if they had our belongings.

I'd just finished my lunch and I was really looking forward to investigating the forest, but first I'd to get past the dinner ladies who were very, very strict.

As I got nearer to the dinner ladies, I saw Eadaoin being shouted at big time, she must have tried to get past the dinner lady the wrong way. Oh no, she's got stood out for five minutes, I'd better go and talk to her to see what she did wrong.

I walked over to Eadaoin and she said 'Go, say to Miss, please let Eadaoin come and play,'
'OK' I answered, so Miss let her come and play.

Quickly and quietly, we sneaked into the forest and began to search until we found a little boy and he said, 'Come with me if you have lost skipping ropes and jumping hoops.'
We followed him until we saw a most fascinating sight, there were all our belongings made into a big climbing frame.

He had used our stuff and trees to make us a secret hideout and that was the kindest thing anyone had ever done for us.

Clare Cummings (9)
St Anne's Primary School, Belfast, Co Antrim

THE OWL AND THE PARROT

One year ago, on a rainy day, there was a man called Mincer. Now Mincer was nice, kind and happy but he hasn't changed a bit.

Mincer was walking home in a storm, when he found an owl on the road. Mincer ran over and took the owl to his house. He said, 'This poor thing is unconscious so I think I'll keep it safe for the night.' He put the owl in a cage next to his parrot. He called the owl, Stormlost and his parrot's name was Repeato.

The next day was sunny and Stormlost and Repeato were hungry. Repeato got some of the usual crackers and Stormlost got some pieces of carrots. Mincer said goodbye as he left to go to work. Repeato then started saying goodbye over and over again. Then Stormlost said, 'Shut you, you stupid parrot.' Then Repeato stopped but started to repeat what Stormlost said, 'Urgghh! Please be quiet Repeato before I fly out of here and get that fork and poke you with it,'
'OK'.
Stormlost gently said, 'I'm trying to go to sleep.'
Repeato stopped and then flew out of the cage, grabbed the fork and Stormlost flinched.
'Repeato said, 'Two for flinching!'
Stormlost flew out of the cage, (Repeato behind) up to a cable and cleverly dodged it. Repeato, instead, flew right into it and got shocked. Repeato hurtled to the ground and said, 'I really sh-sh shouldn't have f-f-flown with a f-f-fork in my claws.'

Stormlost laughed so hard that he started hurtling to the ground, unable to stop. He lay on the ground, laughing in pain. 'You stupid parrot, ha, ha, ha, don't you know that electricity is attracted by metal?' Stormlost laughed.

Mincer came home half an hour later to find his owl and his parrot sleeping in their cage, head to head. 'Awww, I should make both special snacks to repay them for my absence,' Mincer whispered.

Mincer left to go to the kitchen and both birds woke up and Stormlost said, 'It worked, now pretend you're asleep, he's coming back.' The two birds still hate each other today, but a year ago is when it started and when it ends.

I don't know what will happen myself!

Lee Brady (9)
St Anne's Primary School, Belfast, Co Antrim

MY FIRST DAY HUNTING

I have gone back in time to 4000BC and am here to stay.

I got out of my bed and went to join my family to eat my breakfast. When I sat on the ground, I saw that today for breakfast I got a lovely big eel. When I saw it I remembered that today was my birthday! I ate the eel so quickly I nearly choked.

Once I had finished, my uncle said, 'For your birthday, your dad and I are going to take you out hunting.' I was so excited that I ran out of our hut and told all my friends. Then I ran back into our hut, got my clothes on and ran into the room. My mum said to me, 'Here is your birthday present.' I looked at it and started jumping up and down, I couldn't help it, I had got a bow and arrow, all for me.

My dad said, 'Come on for a treat, I'll take you to make your own spear.' I just couldn't believe my luck. Once I had made my spear and had my bow and arrow, we walked towards the forest, now I started to feel scared, the furry animal skin was starting to feel very annoying. I walked closer, my bow and arrow were starting to feel very heavy. I walked closer and was finally in the forest. I walked deeper and deeper into the forest. I kicked a stone by accident and birds flew over my head. I heard heavy thudding hooves running, I jumped and my dad told me to be quiet and watch where I was going or we wouldn't have anything for dinner. I climbed down and walked on down to the side of the forest and there I saw it, a boar.

There was a big, fat boar, I lifted up my bow and arrow and shot. I closed my eyes, slowly I opened them again. I didn't miss, I got it, I walked closer and really felt scared, I didn't want to touch it.

My dad and uncle lifted it. On the way back I saw a really big bird. I lifted up my spear and got it. Then I said, 'I'll lift it' and to my surprise it felt lovely and soft.

When I got back to ours, I told everyone my story, while we had a lovely big dinner.

Christine McGeary (9)
St Anne's Primary School, Belfast, Co Antrim

WUZZLE

One day Professor Bolts For Brains, was trying to cure cancer, but by accident instead of adding copper sulphate he added zinc to the formula crystals. Boom! Professor Bolts For Brains was blasted back to the wall and knocked out. Meanwhile in the test tube a little, red, soft ball had appeared.

'Wuzzle, Wuzzle,' it said in a soft little voice. Professor Bolts For Brains woke up and saw the red little soft ball lying on his T-shirt.

'What the?' he said in a puzzled voice, he picked up the red ball.

'Wuzzle, Wuzzle,' went the little red ball and rolled and rolled and rolled until it made Professor Bolts For Brains dizzy.

'I'll call you Wuzzle,' said Professor Bolts For Brains. He went to his bread cupboard and took out a piece of bread and gave it to Wuzzle. As he ate it, he began to glow. When the glow stopped, there were two Wuzzles.

'You multiplied,' said Professor Bolts For Brains and picked them up.

'I wonder . . . ' he said.

Next day his wife came in and saw about one million Wuzzles.

'We're rich my dear,' said a voice somewhere. Professor Bolts For Brains stood up with Wuzzles all over him. 'We'll sell them for ten pounds each and we'll get millions, I tell you millions!'

Years went by as the Wuzzles multiplied. By now everyone in Ireland had a Wuzzle. Then they sailed to England and on the boat was a sight for sore eyes. They sold the Wuzzles in England. Soon the whole world was packed with Wuzzles and Professor Bolts For Brains and his wife lived in a giant manor with loads of Wuzzles.

Andrew Harris (9)
St Anne's Primary School, Belfast, Co Antrim

SCARY HORROR

One rainy, stormy night, a girl was trying to get to sleep, she heard a banging on the door and a shaking of the window. Then she heard a scream and hid under her bed and there was a pale, white ghost entering her room.

Then ten minutes later, the ghost flew out of the window, then she heard another scream. She started getting really scared and gave a very loud scream, but her parents didn't hear her so she crept out to tell them, but they had been kidnapped by the ghost.

Without any hesitation she went out to search for them but when she got into the woods, the ghost tied her up. That night the ghosts ate them up, so will they become ghosts?

Marc Gribben (9)
St Anne's Primary School, Belfast, Co Antrim

THE EMBARRASSING BROTHER

Hi my name is Tanya and I'm 16 years old, so are all my friends. The only thing is that I have a really annoying, shrimpie five-year-old brother and he can't even say my name right. He calls me Tanie. I hate it, it is so annoying.

When my friends call me on the phone, he comes up to me and starts pulling and picking at my clothes and telling me to play with him and his Tim the teddy. I don't know why he called it Tim, it is an ugly name anyway.

When my mum tells me to clean his room, I put his teddy away in his cupboard and he comes into the room screaming 'No Tanie, no you'll hurt him!' He runs into his room and gets his teddy out of his cupboard with a big, red face, even redder than his jumper, he runs downstairs to tell Mum (after all he is a tell-tale).

So the next day my friend Zoe phoned me and asked me if I could come to the hairdressers with her and I went but what do you know, my brother had to come too.

When we got to the hairdressers, my brother started picking the hairs off the floor and throwing them at the hairdresser. He kept on asking her to cut his hair, but she just kept on saying after this girl. When she said it again, my brother got really mad with her and he started it again, only this time with Zoe's hair. The only thing I could do was take him out of the hairdressers straight away, but when I lifted him, he started kicking and kicking me, 'I want my hair cut!'

When we got out of the hairdressers, he started picking his nose in front of everyone and I was so embarrassed, everyone was looking at us, he probably picked his nose because he was bored.

'I want to go to the toilet' he said. He went into the hairdressers and threw more hair at the hairdressers and went into the girl's bathroom because he didn't like the boys.

He didn't come out for two hours and Zoe was still getting her hair done. When I walked into the hairdressers, I realised that I didn't have to go into the girl's bathroom because he was up at the counter with another girl. I brought him home and told my mum all what he did and he got in trouble (sometimes I can tell too) and he got sent to bed and I got to watch TV. It was great.

Eimear Johnston (9)
St Anne's Primary School, Belfast, Co Antrim

THE THREE PIGS

One day two little pigs were asked to mind Mummy Pig's house. They said yes and they locked the door when Mummy Pig went out.

Fifteen minutes later, there was a knock at the door, Brother Pig unlocked the door and opened it. It was Mummy Pig. Mummy Pig said to Brother Pig 'I have to buy more food, I will be back in half an hour, I'll have a cup of tea first. Oh! That reminds me I have to get tea bags!'

Brother Pig put Baby Sophie to bed for her lunchtime nap. Twenty minutes later, there came a knock at the door, Brother Pig thought Mummy Pig was home early.

Brother Pig opened the door, at the door, was a big, bad, ugly, hairy wolf. He said 'It's lunch and you're a pig, a pig is on the menu!'

At that moment, Mother Pig pulled her car up the drive and saw the wolf and she dropped her shopping and ran up to the back of the wolf (and by the time the wolf was in the house) she hit him with her handbag and he was knocked out.

Then Mother Pig and Brother Pig lifted the wolf and threw him into the boiling water and he was killed.

Mother Pig never left Brother Pig and baby Sophie in the house alone again and they lived happily ever after.

Nicole Elliman (9)
St Anne's Primary School, Belfast, Co Antrim

MY VERSION OF THE THREE LITTLE PIGS

Far into the woods, in a little cottage there lived three pigs and their mother. The three little pigs names were Edward, Justin and Henry.

One day their mother told them to go to live in their own houses, there weren't many things that the pigs owned, so they left early.

By the next day, they had built their houses and they were cosy. The two brothers of Edward came to see his brick house.

The very next day, a wolf knocked on Justin's door but Justin wouldn't let him in. The wolf said, 'I'll huff and I'll puff and blow your house down.'

The pig got out of the house as fast as he could, he ran off to Edward's house, on the way he stopped off at Henry's and told him to come too.

Back at Edward's, the pigs prepared a trap at the front door. When the wolf rang the doorbell, the trap fell on him.

The next day the pigs tied the wolf to the train tracks and went home. When they returned they found a dead body.

Philip Kielt (9)
St Anne's Primary School, Belfast, Co Antrim

THIS IS MY VERSION OF THE STORY OF THE THREE PIGS

There once were three little pigs and their names were Oinky, Porky and Smarty. They had each built a house. Oinky had built a house made out of straw, Porky had made his out of sticks and Smarty had made his out of bricks.

One day, Oinky, Porky and Smarty went out for walk in the woods. They found a small patch under a tree so they had their lunch.

They started to walk home when they saw the wolf coming their way. They quickly ran behind some bushes so that the wolf could not eat them. When the wolf had gone, they ran home as fast as they could.

Smarty invited Porky and Oinky for dinner so they came over. In the middle of dinner, there was a knock at the door so Smarty went to answer it. He thought it was their mother, but it was the wolf so Smarty opened the door and the wolf ate him. After the wolf had eaten Smarty, he went home. The two brothers came out to see what was taking Smarty so long, when they got to the door Smarty had disappeared.

Porky and Oinky went back to Porky's house and telephoned their mother to tell her what had happened, so they had made a plan for the next time the wolf came to try and eat them.

The wolf came the next night to try and eat the pigs but they did not let him in, so the wolf came through the chimney and started chasing the pigs round the house. The wolf did not get the pigs because when the wolf was chasing Porky around the house, Oinky phoned the pig police and the police came and took the wolf away.

Oinky and Porky lived together happily because there was no wolf to try and eat them and they went to see Smarty's grave every day and their mum too.

Kate Collins (9)
St Anne's Primary School, Belfast, Co Antrim

FRIENDLY VISITED

One sunny morning, the bell rang while we were outside playing. We went into the class and started work. There was a knock on the door, my teacher told me to open the door, I opened the door and there was something in front of me. My teacher had planned a dressed up funny man to come to our class and dance for us but it was not that man. My friend Katie said it was a Martian. All my friends had fainted except for me and Katie. My teacher ran out of the class saying 'Ahhh.'

The Martian was all different colours, pink stripes, green stripes, all the colours you could think of. We sat down, we started to talk, me and Katie thought he was cool but really he only came for a visit.

We went to the cinema, bowling and ice skating, the Martian had so much fun, he wanted to stay, I dressed him as a girl and said to my mum it was a friend.

We got bacon, egg and prawns for breakfast. All my friends were still lying on the ground in school, in class 2. We went to the town fair, it was so much fun, we ate candyfloss and we went on the roller coaster.

The Martian wanted to go places by himself, so I went and brought some balloons and some new clothes. I met the Martian again, he said he saw a sign on the lamp post that there was going to be a party.

Me and the Martian went to the party, we were having so much fun until the Martian said, 'Come I want to show you my planet that I live on.'

His planet had a big black hole in it and outside several stripes. The Martian had to go home but at the weekend's he said he would come back.

Rebecca McMahon (9)
St Anne's Primary School, Belfast, Co Antrim

A GHOST STORY

Lucy Marten, aged eight, was a member of a big family. She was one of eight children and her mum was expecting twins! Clearly their house was not going to be big enough for twelve people so they finished up moving to a larger home in London. Some people said that strange things happened in that house but Lucy did not believe in ghosts . . . until the day she entered the back bedroom at the far end of the upstairs passage.

Lucy pushed open the creaking door to find a shabbily dressed child looking out of the window. She held a rag doll in her hand. She turned away from the window and placed the doll in a faded, tattered shoulder bag that had been patched and re-patched many times. Flames licked the sky and buildings burned on the other side of that window.

'I am Hannah Marten,' said the girl. 'It is the year 1666 and London is burning.'

Lucy was shocked to hear this. She had the same name as Hannah. Perhaps they were related, she thought. The girls talked for an hour about each other. Lucy realised that she had gone back in time to the Great Fire. Hannah began to fade away and everything in the room returned to normal.

Deirbhile Carson (8)
St Anne's Primary School, Belfast, Co Antrim

A GHOST STORY

I first became aware of my nocturnal neighbours the first night I slept in my new house. I had been in bed for just ten minutes when the noises began next door. Strange, I thought. Nobody had lived in that house for months. Maybe burglars. Should I call the police? But the house was empty. There was nothing in there worth stealing.

Next morning the noises were still going through my head. I phoned my brother to ask him to stay the night. The noises began that night. I put my hands over my ears to block out the sound. Luckily my brother heard everything. We decided that in the morning we would investigate that house.

We forced open the back door and tiptoed upstairs to the bedroom next to my room. Pushing open the door we could see several figures sitting at a table. They were laughing and playing cards, but they were *ghosts!* At least they were friendly to us.

Now they are our friends and my brother and I visit them often. The night noises no longer frighten me as I now know what causes them.

Katie Wallace (8)
St Anne's Primary School, Belfast, Co Antrim

A DAY IN THE LIFE OF CASPER (THE FRIENDLY DOG)

I remember well the day I met Lauren and the rest of her family. I just knew that life was going to be a lot of more fun. They bought me from a pet shop. At first I was quite scared when the cage door opened but I walked slowly out to meet my new family.

'Oh, he's lovely,' Lauren called out excitedly. 'What's his name?'

But a little dog like me didn't have a name. The family came up with many suggestions - Snowy? Ben? Casper? They settled on Casper even though I would have preferred 'Ben' but I didn't really mind.

Back home and dinner was already in my bowl. Yummy! Then into the garden to play fetch the ball. 'Get the ball. Run boy. Oops, don't drop it,' the children screamed at me. This was great fun and I wanted to play all night but soon it was time for bed. Yawn. I am kinda tired. Tucked in, blanket over me. Kick, kick. I'm too warm. Blanket off now. Too excited. Can't sleep. Too many thoughts. Calm down. Try to sleep. Is that the breakfast dishes I hear? Another day begins. I can't wait!

Lauren Cunningham (8)
St Anne's Primary School, Belfast, Co Antrim

A GHOST STORY

It was a dark, dark stormy night with lightning forking across the sky. Tom was driving carefully through the rain wishing to be at home again. Suddenly, in his car headlights, he spied what looked like a body lying at the side of the road. He stopped the car with a screech of brakes and went out to have a look. Getting closer to the body he saw that it was a little girl covered in pieces of grass and nettles. His first thought was to run back to the car to get the blanket in the boot. On his return he found the girl had disappeared. Thinking that perhaps she was alive and had rolled under the bushes, he began a search but found nothing. He drove home as quickly as possible and told his wife all that had happened.

Tom did not sleep well. He woke up in the middle of the night to see the little girl standing in the room. He woke up his wife to tell her but then she disappeared again.

At breakfast next morning Tom decided that he would try to find out about this mysterious girl. In old newspapers he found out that a girl had died at the place where he had first seen the body. That was ten years ago. Now he had proof.

Rachael Flanagan (8)
St Anne's Primary School, Belfast, Co Antrim

A Day In The Life Of Mae

The day I met Lucy I knew that she would love me. After all, I am so soft and cuddly. She came with her family to the pound in Lisburn where I lived. One look at me and I was sure that she would take me home.

They decided to call me Mae because they got me in the mouth of May. When I arrived at Lucy's home I knew that I was going to have a great time there. Lucy took me on a lead out into the garden. So much space to run about in. Many exciting new smells for a dog to explore. Lucy could sense that I wanted to have some fun so she let me off the lead. Away I went up the garden charging about at great speed. Lucy was watching my antics which made her laugh out loud. I was thinking happy thoughts because I had made her laugh. She picked me up and kissed me and she told me that it was nearly time for bed. I didn't mind because I was very tired. I was going to enjoy being tucked into my basket by Lucy. I knew that we were going to have very many happy days together.

Lucy Torney (8)
St Anne's Primary School, Belfast, Co Antrim

THE ROPE BRIDGE

One day I was out playing when a man and a woman grabbed me and put tape around my mouth, then threw me roughly in their car. They started to laugh and I heard them saying that they would sell me for 2,000 pounds. I was so frightened, I thought I would never see my mummy and daddy again.

At last they stopped the car and the man threw me out, then I kicked him on the shin until he let me go. I ran away terrified. I ran and ran until I came to an old bridge. This was the only thing that would allow me to cross the deep canyon below and to escape from my kidnappers.

Some planks on the bridge were missing, then it started to rain and the wind blew heavily. I was terrified. The rope began to shake so hard that the logs were breaking. Then I fell, but I got back up again and I luckily got off the bridge.

I saw a town in front of me so I went off looking for the police. When I looked back I saw the kidnappers running towards me but I was near to the police station. I told the police what had happened and the kidnappers were put in jail.

Rose Smyth (8)
St Anne's Primary School, Belfast, Co Antrim

THE PLANE CRASH

On the day my family and I were flying over France when a storm started. I was so petrified that I clenched onto my dad. A bolt of lightning hit one of the plane's wings and it fell off. The pilot said to the people to keep calm and prepare for a crash landing. I was so frightened, my mum had to help me move.

When the plane crashed my family and I were lucky to survive. Unfortunately people died and others were severely injured. I said to my dad to ring the rescue service but his mobile's battery was flat. We were panic-stricken.

My dad and I decided we would go and get help while my sister and mum stayed to help the injured.

My dad and I had to cross a bridge. I was really anxious in case I fell but I knew we had to go across it. We were halfway over the bridge when it started swaying. My dad and I knew we had to be careful because we could fall over the edge. When we were nearly there, suddenly a plank of wood that I stepped on broke and I fell down. Luckily my dad caught me - I was so glad I had my dad with me.

When my dad and I reached a village we looked for a telephone. We found one and phoned the rescue services and told them where the plane had crashed.

Patrick Cunningham (9)
St Anne's Primary School, Belfast, Co Antrim

THE BIG OLD BRIDGE

My mum has won £100,000 from the Lotto and our picture was on the front of the newspaper, and this is where my troubles began.

A man was walking and saw the newspaper. He saw our picture and also saw that we had won £100,000. He kidnapped me and took me up the mountain to where he lived. He then rang my parents and said, 'I want £100,000, or you will never see your daughter again.'

That night I arrived on the mountain and I was scared, but I knew I had to escape. Beside me there was a table and on top of it was a knife. I got the knife and cut the rope which was tied around my hands. The door was not locked so I ran out. I was scared being all alone on the mountain. I ran along until I came to a bridge. The sun was coming up and I saw that the rope was old and frayed. I knew I had to cross the bridge so I started walking across. I was very scared and I was shaking, but I knew I had to cross it.

When I was halfway over I slipped and I was holding on to the bridge with my hands. I managed to pull myself back up. Soon I got to the other side. I felt happy but I saw that I had to climb another bridge, so I started climbing down. When I got to the ground I ran to the other mountain and started climbing. I was halfway up it and it was turning dark, I kept climbing though. Soon it was midnight and I was near the top, so I climbed a bit more. I reached the top and I was very happy. I then went to sleep.

Next morning I got up and started to climb down. It was a very long journey going down the mountain but soon I reached the bottom. I saw lots of trees and I ran through them. When I got through I saw a town. I knew I was home so I started to run. I got home and rang the doorbell. My mum and dad answered and they were both very happy to see me. I was happy to see them too.

Stephenie McKenna (9)
St Anne's Primary School, Belfast, Co Antrim

My Great Escape From Alcatraz

I was escaping from Alcatraz. I looked anxiously back. I saw seventeen guards with torches blazing full blast. I was petrified. The guards were hot on my heels, it was as if I could feel them breathing down my neck.

I came across a rocky mountain face. I saw a rope bridge, its rope looked frayed. The guards were still on the chase. It was now or never, I had to cross this dangerous rope bridge. I did not want another eleven years in Alcatraz. I counted down from ten - 10, 9, 8, 7, 6, 5, 4, 3, 2 . . . this was it . . . 1. I ran then slipped. I was hanging on by my fingertips. Now I was sweating everywhere. I put all my energy into pulling myself up. Luckily I lifted myself back onto my feet. I was back up once again and the guards were now coming nearer. I needed to get over the bridge. I ran, blood shot across the rope bridge. I finally reached the other side. Yes! Now all I had to do was run down towards the shore where I saw a boat. My luck couldn't have been better. I boarded the boat; no paddles - my luck had run out but it didn't matter. I used my hands. I took one last look back at the island and I didn't see one guard; I'd lost them. This was my great escape and I was the first person to escape from Alcatraz.

James McKee (9)
St Anne's Primary School, Belfast, Co Antrim

THE BRIDGE

My grandad was very sick and he was going to die. I had heard that there was a yellow flower on the mountain but I had to cross a rope bridge to get the flower. I had left a note to let my mummy and daddy know that I was going on the quest to get the flower.

I was afraid because I heard that lots of people had died because they had fallen off this rope bridge. But I knew I had to cross it. I slowly put my foot on the first step and I moved very slowly. Then I finally reached the end of the bridge. I ran to get the medicine. Now I had to cross this treacherous bridge again. I was afraid. I went very slowly, very slowly and when I reached the middle of the bridge one of the planks fell off and my foot slipped. I was just about to fall but I managed to steady myself again. I walked slowly over the rest of the bridge. I ran over to my grandad's house. He was just about to die but I gave him the medicine and saved him. I was so proud that I'd saved his life and that I had crossed that treacherous bridge, not once but twice.

Amy Murray (9)
St Anne's Primary School, Belfast, Co Antrim

MY ESCAPE ACROSS THE DANGEROUS BRIDGE

My sister and I had just won the lottery and were on our way to a party when all of a sudden I heard a noise. I turned round but Janice wasn't there. I shouted, 'Janice very funny, we're going to miss the party!' I shouted again but still no answer. There was a gust of wind and there, at my feet, was a letter. It said, 'If you want to see your sister again, go to the mountains and bring your lotto winnings.'

At first I thought, this is weird, but I really loved my sister so I went anyway. I rode up through the mountains on my bike until I came to a thin ledge. I was scared stiff, but I edged my way along.

I came to a rope bridge (it was old and frayed and very dangerous) and there I met the man who kidnapped my sister.

'Where's my money?' he shouted. He had a gun so I handed over the bag. I grabbed my sister by the hand and started running across the old bridge. My sister slipped and I helped her up. My heart was beating like mad. It was raining hard now and I was so scared. Suddenly a plank fell far below and I was hanging on for dear life by my fingertips. With Janice's help I managed to get up.

We ran down hill and caught a bus from there but my sister said, 'Why did you give him the money?'
'I didn't,' I said. 'I made fake money and we have the real money to spend for ourselves.'

Laura Hughes (9)
St Anne's Primary School, Belfast, Co Antrim

LIFE AS A MESOTHIC CHILD

My name is Moosasa and I have just arrived at this new place along the river. I've just been on a boat for many days with my family and I am really tired and hungry. I can't wait until I go and get the hazel rods to make our hut and we will use the deer skin we bought to cover the rods.

My dad and brother went hunting and they bought bows and arrows with them. I hope they will bring back a wild boar. My mum and sister went to pick huts and berries. I am collecting rods for the hut while my family is away. When my family is back we will light the fire and whatever my dad kills, my mum will cook it over the spit.

Christopher Hyndman (9)
St Anne's Primary School, Belfast, Co Antrim

MY ESCAPE FROM THE ALIENS

I recently became an orphan. My parents had died in a plane crash - or so I thought. Deep down I think they're still alive. I think this is just a cover up. The 'authorities' hated my parents; they had found out that the 'authorities' were aliens (hard to believe I know) trying to take over the world. Then suddenly the phone went. At first I thought it was someone from the town saying how sympathetic they were, but it was the town mayor. He said I had to live with foster parents. He went on to say that if I didn't comply, I would be chucked out of the city (better than foster parents, I thought.)

I wanted to swear down the phone at him in anger, but I just put it down. Half of me said, escape, run away, but the other side said, 'Nah, it won't be that bad,' but it was. In the weeks to come, it wasn't bad at all, it was worse, worse than worse, too difficult to describe. I got up at 6.00 every morning to make them a very nice breakfast. I won't tell you what I had to do in the afternoon, you wouldn't like it.

So anyway, I had started to plan my escape. I would take my dad's rucksack, get all the food it could hold, and of course drinks, and at 12.30am (my foster family go to bed at 12.00) I would climb through the window and on to find my mum and dad. While I was climbing through the window I thought I should take a bike because someone might see me and wonder what I was doing. When I got to the bike shop I saw that they were still open, which was weird. I wanted to get closer, so I hid behind a barrel near the door. I only heard a few words of what two people in the shop were saying, but it sounded clear enough. 'Yes, they have no idea what we're doing, the planet will be ours by next week!'
'Uh, those darn alien scumbags,' I whispered. When they were gone I slid in and took the best bike there was.

I travelled across mountains for what seemed like hours, sun blazing. I was exhausted and thirsty (all my rations were gone.) Suddenly the mountain road seemed to fade, and then I came across a bridge. No, not the bridges we have nowadays, a rope bridge, a terrible rope bridge may I add. Some of the planks were missing and it started to rain. I edged closer to the bridge and stepped onto the first plank. Not bad, I thought.

But I had twenty more planks to go. Now I had to jump to the next plank because there was a gap. I started to walk a bit quicker and eventually I got there. A sense of relief followed me as I continued the journey to find my mum and dad.

Philip Kennedy (9)
St Anne's Primary School, Belfast, Co Antrim

THE GREAT ESCAPE

When I was playing with my friends it started to get stormy, so all of my friends went indoors. While I was walking home a man pulled me into his car. I was frightened and the man said, 'Your dad wanted me to pick you up.' I tried to get out of the car but I couldn't because the car doors were locked. I was terrified as the man drove off.

He brought me to the top of a mountain and opened the car door. That was my chance, I could run. I ran down the mountain and then came to a rope bridge. I was frightened. I stood on the third step. I went onto the next and it broke. Somehow I managed to get up again, then I got back. I hugged my mum and dad. I was so happy that I was back safely.

Claire Lewsley (9)
St Anne's Primary School, Belfast, Co Antrim

THE GREAT ESCAPE

My name is Johnny Crock. I work for a secret Mafia gang. When I was stealing valuable jewels from a jewellery shop, the police saw me. I managed to escape but they chased me in their car. The boss of the Mafia told me to head out of the city in a car and go north to a mountain. It was here I would exchange the money for the jewels. I looked back and saw that I had lost the cops. I can remember the boss of the Mafia told me there was a rope bridge high up on the mountain for me to cross.

When I got to the top of the mountain I came to a standstill. There in front of me was a very old rope bridge I would have to go across. I walked across the first few steps and then I was alarmed when I saw the frayed wire and that some wooden planks were broken and some were missing. I saw that the cops had caught up with me so I started to walk. One of the cops was comng towards me but the bridge fell in the middle and the cop fell off. I was still hanging onto the bit of rope tied to a log of wood. When I got up I saw the open road and on the other side was the Mafia gang.

Domhnall McHugh (9)
St Anne's Primary School, Belfast, Co Antrim

THE GREAT ESCAPE

I was coming back from visiting my cousins in America, when suddenly the plane crashed. Some of us were injured. It was worse than we thought because the only place we could go to get help was across the rope bridge - a dangerous rope bridge, with water and rocks at the bottom.

We needed help so badly, someone had to cross the treacherous rope bridge and that person was me! I started to walk along the bridge, but then a plank of wood dropped in front of me and it was starting to rain. It was a storm. I could hardly see while I was walking across it. the bridge was getting slippery, I almost fell off.

I was terrified, but before I knew it, I was over the bridge. The storm was getting worse. I had to walk two more miles to get to the town. At last, I got help for the injured people and instead of walking across the bridge, I got a helicopter back.

Catherine Austin (9)
St Anne's Primary School, Belfast, Co Antrim

THE ROPE BRIDGE

One day, I was out playing with my friend and two men came towards us. All my friends ran away, but I didn't. The two men grabbed me and took me on a long journey.

As the man opened his car boot, I kicked him in the knee and escaped. I ran as fast as I could. Suddenly, I came to a rope bridge. The two men came chasing after me. I had no choice but to cross the bridge. As I crossed the bridge, I noticed that the ropes were frayed and some planks were missing. I got across the bridge and then I ran to the police station. I got there and told them all about my kidnapping.

The police caught the bad guys and put them in jail. Then the police rang my mum and dad and they came down to the police station. I was glad to see Mum and Dad again.

Caoimhe Drain (8)
St Anne's Primary School, Belfast, Co Antrim

THE DEADLY BRIDGE

My sister and I are running away from the town because my sister's old boyfriend has just robbed a bank and he wants her to hide the money. We saw the robbery on the news, now we are packing our bags and getting into the jeep, before he comes after us to hide the money. We are going to the mountains to hide, but we've run out of petrol.

As we climb over a steep hill, we notice that my sister's old boyfriend is chasing us. He's speeding after us, we're petrified. Our hands are shaking, we are sweating as we step onto the dangerous bridge. The bridge is swaying harder and harder, and it's starting to rain. We are sweating more and more; my sister's old boyfriend is catching us. Each time we step on a plank, it creaks and we are sweating more and more.

'Arghhhh!' we cry together because the last ten planks have fallen. My sister and I have to jump if we want to escape. One, two, three, four, five, six, seven, eight, nine, ten! We jump and make it. Now my sister's old boyfriend has turned around and is heading back to town.

Conor McCourt (9)
St Anne's Primary School, Belfast, Co Antrim

MY GREAT ESCAPE

I had just escaped from prison in the search for £1,000,000 stolen from the bank and hidden in a cave. The guards were after me with tracker dogs and my only getaway was an old, tatty rope bridge with frayed ropes and missing and broken planks. The bridge was over a deep canyon and I really didn't want to cross it, but I knew that I must, so I started across. Suddenly, the sky grew dark and the wind blew very hard and the bridge began to sway. The guards were now at the bridge. They stopped and stared at me, now I grew even more scared because I thought the guards would send the dogs after me. I collected my thoughts and continued on, then I slipped and I was hanging on by my fingertips. I was sweating like mad, but luckily I got back up.

Finally I got across, then quickly grabbed a sharp stone and cut the ropes so the guards couldn't cross. After that, I managed to find the money and now I'm rich and relieved to have got across that bridge, but the cops are still out looking for me.

Guilhaume McAllister (9)
St Anne's Primary School, Belfast, Co Antrim

THE PLANE CRASH

I was travelling alone for the first time to meet my family in America. I boarded the plane and I was excited about seeing my family again. Not long after take-off, the plane crashed. Most people were hurt, but I was lucky not to be. Since I was the only one fit, I went to get help.

As I was walking along, I came to a dangerous rope bridge. I knew there was a town across the bridge on the other side. I knew I had to cross it.

As I was crossing it, the bridge was swaying. I was shaking and very scared. Many of the laths were broken and that made it harder to cross. My body was trembling and my heart was pumping. I finally got to the other side. I was so relieved, I had crossed the bridge and I was exhausted. I started to walk to the town where I could get help. This time, I didn't go over the bridge, I got a helicopter back to the plane crash site.

Lyndsey McClune (9)
St Anne's Primary School, Belfast, Co Antrim

THE GREAT ESCAPE

One day I was out playing in the street when I found a bag with three million pounds in it. Suddenly, a man came by and said, 'What do you have there, little girl?'

I said, 'Three million pounds.'

He said, 'Give it to me.'

I said, 'No.'

Then he kidnapped me. I was screaming like mad, so he stuffed a cloth into my mouth and shoved me into the boot of a car. I still had the three million pounds. He took me to the mountains and tied me up and took the money and left me up on the mountain.

Much later I escaped and I ran as fast as I could, until I came to a rope bridge. The rope bridge was very old and the rope was frayed and the laths were broken and some were hanging down. Unluckily for me, it wasn't a calm day. It started to pour and soon a storm broke out. Next thing, I saw the man coming. I didn't know what way to go, then I stepped onto the bridge, trembling with fear.

The bridge was swaying in the wind. The man was coming closer and closer, he was shouting 'Come back here!' I didn't look back. Well, would you if you were on an old, frayed, broken bridge that was over a 20ft drop down to a rocky canyon? I took another few steps, then a big gust of wind came and the bridge nearly tipped over with me on it. As I tried to go a bit faster, I broke one of the laths and I fell through it. I was holding on with my hand. I felt my hand slipping, I steadied the bridge and pulled myself up. I finally got across the bridge. I heard the man fall down, but he was still hanging on, though the three million pounds had dropped, but I didn't care anymore. I ran down the hill, not looking back, and ran

When I got home, I told my mummy about the three million pounds, the man and the rope bridge. She just said, 'You've been daydreaming again!'

Anna Crossan (9)
St Anne's Primary School, Belfast, Co Antrim

DEAD CHILDREN

Everything appeared normal the day that it happened. I was walking past a derelict house on my way home when I saw him - a child in the window of the house, with eyes like pearls and skin the colour of mist. Slowly, he raised his bloodless hand and waved. I decided to go and explore. I climbed the crumbling steps, almost tripping on the withered ivy and pushed open the massive wooden, creaking doors.

He stood there beckoning me forwards and up the dusty stairs. I started to climb the stairs, pulling the cobwebs from my face and clothes. I followed him down a dark and dismal corridor into a large, icy room. The stench was unbearable, the floor was covered with decaying bodies of boys. I realised I had to run for my life. Knowing that speed was critical, I raced back the way I came. Slipping on moss, I skidded back to where it started.

Would my mum believe me? I don't think so. In future, I'm going straight home.

Christopher Madden (11)
St Anne's Primary School, Rosemount, Co Londonderry

THE TALE OF THE ARCHWAY FACTORY

She paused a second and looked at the remains of the old Archway Factory. Kate Weatherfield had heard strange stories of this building from her friends, but she never took them on, and tonight, since she was staying at her granny's until 10:30pm, she planned to find out the truth.

She headed through the wooden door covered in graffiti, on her own because her friend refused to go. She passed twelve deathly black rooms until she reached it, the thirteenth room on the thirteenth floor. Now just thirteen minutes until she is proven right.

Kate was feeling nervous now as she heard strange humming noises coming from behind. She glanced at the room again and noticed a bright figure of a working woman appearing. Kate soon realised that she was standing in front of a *ghost!* Kate thought the face looked familiar as it turned to her and gave her a locket with the woman's photo inside. Kate then suddenly found herself back in her bed thinking it was all a dream, before finding the locket around her neck. She resembled that photo of her grandma's and realised that she was the spirit of the ghost she saw last night.

Stephanie Bradley (11)
St Anne's Primary School, Rosemount, Co Londonderry

A Day In The Life Of My Teacher!

Well, my teacher starts off his day by coming into school and asking for homework, and then you see, he is bound to make a scene like this!
'Declan, what is 40 x 4?'
'Ah, 165.'
'Oh Declan, you goat's toe!'
And you'll be sitting there praying, please don't pick on me next.

Next on his daily schedule, 'Don't give sympathy for pain.' Here is a good way to describe this. Everyone is doing their work and Aveen falls off her chair and he starts to laugh. I reckon he has to take pride in himself by being non-sympathetic.

Our class is glad when it is lunchtime, when we get away from him, but then down in the dumps when it's homework time, when he goes, 'You'll like the homework,' and a sudden groan comes from the class.

The moral of the story is, avoid Mr B Bradley.

Eoghan Nelis (11)
St Anne's Primary School, Rosemount, Co Londonderry

A DAY IN THE LIFE OF A DOG

Hello! My name is Rover and I am a King Charles spaniel. My owners think I'm cute, cuddly and playful, but they don't know the real me. Every morning after I scoff down my breakfast and lap up my milk, I scramble out of the garden and sniff around for any scent of my enemy, who is the postman. Postmen are my greatest enemies, apart from cats. Each and every single morning, I growl at and chase the postman the whole way down the street while he shouts and screams. I snap playfully at his heels, but he thinks I'm trying to bite his whole leg off!

I usually take a nap after the chase. I lay lazily in the sun, drool slipping from my mouth. When I wake up, I chew happily on my dinner and then have fun trying to chase my next door neighbour's cat. Usually, I can't catch him as he is very fast, but sometimes I do. Dinnertime! I think to myself.

Aisling O'Neill (11)
St Anne's Primary School, Rosemount, Co Londonderry

APRIL FOOL IN LIVERPOOL

Tim was going to Liverpool to meet his cousins. The next day, his father took him to the airport. He got on the plane a few hours later. Soon after the plane took off, a man stood up and pulled out a gun. He then said, 'Everyone, give me all your money.' He went round all the people, collecting their money. Eventually, he came to Tim who left his wallet in his suitcase. The man pulled Tim off his seat, held the gun to his head and dragged him into the cockpit. He said to the pilot, 'I want one million pounds waiting for me at the airport, or else I will kill this boy.'

When they got to Liverpool, the plane landed and the man dragged Tim off the plane and into the airport. then in the airport, the man shouted at Tim, *'April fool!'* and that instant, Tim noticed the man was his uncle he was going to meet.

John Harley (11)
St Anne's Primary School, Rosemount, Co Londonderry

MICHAEL JACKSON

Hi, my name is Michael Jackson. I do not sleep in a real bed, I sleep in a phyboractive chamber. When I get up, I go over the to recording studio to make the video which I am working on. I make up new actions on the new song. Maybe if it's a smooth surface, I can do the moonwalk in the video.

I then record my song on the TV to see what it looks like. If my boss does not like what he sees, he will make me do more practice on the video. When I have finished my song, I will release an album, then I will go on concerts to promote it. I will be nervous, but I have to do it because all my fans are there, screaming and shouting, 'Michael, Michael, Michael.'
This is what I do.

Aaron McCusker (11)
St Anne's Primary School, Rosemount, Co Londonderry

FAMILY AND FRIENDS

My name is Jacqueline Shiels. I am writing about my friends and family.

When I was young, I had lots of friends, but when I moved into primary one, I got more friends like Meghan, Michaela, Soraya and Nicole. My street is called Glenowen. I have met more people like Caoimhe, Rachael, Sasha, Jd, Paul. Even though Jd and Sasha are my cousins, they are still my friends. All my cousins are my friends. My friends take care of me and share with me.

This is about my family. My mum is called Mary, my dad is called Daniel, my brother is called Thomas and my sister is called Sinead. My family are loving, caring and kind. My family have done lots of things for me. They got me a home and a great life and that's why I love my friends and family.

Jacqueline Shiels (11)
St Anne's Primary School, Rosemount, Co Londonderry

WHAT WILL WE DO?

'We'll take the bridge and town to stop the Germans advancing towards central Europe. This battle will be crucial to me, now I need everyone to be at their best,' said Col Rainman.

'I am with you sir,' replied Cpt Roberts, and soon many soldiers of the garrison were involved.

'OK, Roberts, I want you and your men collected and fighting on the bridge. Johnson, I want you in that church tower watching over us, the rest of you collect what ammo you can, find your own positions,' said the Colonel with a satisfied grin.

It was Wednesday, 15th May. The soldiers were vervous and were unsure of the outcome.

'So, what do you think's gonna happen, Captain?' said the nervous private.

'I am not sure. We're in the hands of the Colonel,' replied the captain.

Tension was high between the ranks and morale was low. Suddenly, the rumble of Nazi tanks was in the air.

'Take your positions!' shouted the colonel.

The men scrambled to their positions. Nazi soldiers surrounding the tank, machine guns were roaring as the Nazis launched the assault. After six days of intense fighting, the Germans could take no more and surrendered.

The soldiers celebrated. 'Three cheers for the Colonel!' they cried.

Paul Gill (11)
St Anne's Primary School, Rosemount, Co Londonderry

My Confirmation Day

On the 16th of April, I made my confirmation. This was a very special day for me and my family. On that mass, I got peace, love, joy, patience, kindness, goodness, truthfulness, gentleness and self-control. Near the end of the mass I made my confirmation pledge to not drink until I am eighteen and I will never smoke or take drugs.

After the mass, my family took pictures of me and we got to get a picture with the priest. Then we went for a meal down in the Strand Bar. I got a lot of money, but I know it's not about money. It is about making an important sacrament and receiving the Holy Spirit.

Aaron McDaid (10)
St Anne's Primary School, Rosemount, Co Londonderry

HORROR FILM

One night, my friend Amy and I were walking home after seeing a horror film at the cinema. We were running late so we decided to take a shortcut across a dark lane. I turned round to talk to Amy, but she had vanished like magic. I thought she was playing a joke, so I walked on. I heard footsteps behind me so I turned round thinking I would see Amy, but no one was there. I called out her name, but the only reply I got was my call echoing in the wind.

I was not going to let Amy scare me. I quickened my pace, as it was a cold and stormy night. The leaves rustled in the trees all around me and I had to hold my hat so it would not blow away in the storm.

When I reached her house the front door creaked open; I went into the front room where I found the television playing to itself. I could not find anyone anywhere and I began to get scared. I heard a voice calling for help and I thought it sounded like Amy. I went over to turn off the television so I could hear better. When I looked up at the screen, to my horror, I saw Amy and her family trapped . . .

Eimear O'Donnell (11)
St Anne's Primary School, Rosemount, Co Londonderry

GHOST STORY

One night it was coming into the winter when Sharon went out for a night on the town. Sharon and her friends were having a laugh, but when it got really late they decided to go on home. The went to the taxi stand but they were told it would be forty-five minutes before the next taxi would be available, so they decided to walk on up to Sharon's house.

Everything was going fine until they noticed a very tall and dark figure walking up behind them. They thought nothing of it and just carried on walking and talking. When they got just a little frightened, they started to walk a little more briskly, when they noticed the tall and dark figure behind them was walking faster as well.

Sharon's house is positioned in quite an enclosed area with only about twelve houses, so when the tall and dark figure came right up into Sharon's street, they were very scared. When Sharon and her friends got into Sharon's house, they decided to look out of the window and see if the tall and dark figure was still standing there. They noticed he was floating, but they thought it was just an illusion and to this day, it is still a mystery unsolved.

Christina Hamilton (11)
St Anne's Primary School, Rosemount, Co Londonderry

A DAY IN THE LIFE OF BRITNEY SPEARS

Today, I got up at 7.30am and went for a jog with my dog. My dog started to get very excited when a man and his dog walked by. I was afraid the other dog might bite her, so we retired and went back to my house. I then had a shower which I enjoyed very much.

Next I got a call form my agent saying that he wanted to me to go for an interview with 'Now' magazine, who wanted me for an article on one of my new songs. (I'm Not A girl, Not Yet A Woman.) Then I went to a swimming pool where I met my best friend, Jane. We then went to the beauty parlour where I got my make-up done and my hair done, then the Jacuzzi, followed by the steam room.

Soon after, I went to the recording studio to record my new song. It took one hour to complete the single properly. After this very busy day, I went home to see my dog, who I was glad to see. Then I decided to rent a video, so I went to the video store where I got my video and sweets, (of course I couldn't forget the sweets.) so me and my dog curled up in front of the fire and watched television.

Emily McGlinchey (11)
St Anne's Primary School, Rosemount, Co Londonderry

A Day In The Life Of Rachel Stevens

Hello, my name is Rachel Stevens and I am in S Club 7. Today the band and I have to go to meet our manager at lunchtime, but now most of us are having a lie-in, except for me, Bradley and Jo. At 11:15, everyone was up and ready to go, so we started to walk to the coffee shop.

When we got there, our manager was already there waiting and he said that we had to record our new album, so he gave us a lift to the recording studio. We were recording our album in the studio for four or five hours. After we had finished recording, we went out for our dinner. We had to rush, because we had to perform our concert at the Point Theatre in Dublin.

When we got there, we had to go in and get our make-up done, our hair done too, and we put on new clothes. And in what seemed like no time at all, the concert started. The turn at the concert was amazing, I did not know we had so many fans.

After the concert, we had a couple of backstage passes. The people who had backstage passes only stayed for about twenty minutes. When we got home, I stayed up for about half an hour and then I went to bed.

Clair Loughrey (11)
St Anne's Primary School, Rosemount, Co Londonderry

DON'T DREAM, JUST SCREAM

Monday, 10th July 1845

Dear diary, I was at school when my friend Josh ran in.
'Sir, the potatoes are rotting in the ground! What will we do, Sir?'
'Go home and help,' said Mr McDaid.
We ran home as fast as our legs would carry us.

When I got home, I saw Dad on his hunkers beside the potato crops. I ran over. 'Dad, we can still get a few out.'
'It's no use, son.'

That night, I went to see if I could catch dinner. I came back with a fish which we ate nicely with our last six potatoes. I went to bed with no supper. I had unsuitable nightmares.

I woke next morning and went downstairs and at the foot of the stairs was my father. Well, I'm in for another horrible day tomorrow.

Seámus Clarke (11)
St Anne's Primary School, Rosemount, Co Londonderry

THE GREEN LADY

On the twenty-first of August, a young girl was found dead on the shore of a beach in Peru. People said she drowned herself, but the people of Peru said she was murdered by a lady. This lady was called the Green Lady. She was said to go around and kill children the same age as her beloved daughter, Kay. Kay was killed outside her grandma's house in Mexico, aged eight.

After two more murders in Peru, people at once believed in the Green Lady. They started to worry.

After two more murders in Peru, the Green Lady appeared in Ireland. She was said to be seen walking magically across the River Foyle in Derry City and to be seen running wild in gardens where many children play. One child was killed in her garden in Belfast. It is still not known how, but many think it was her, the Green Lady. She vanished for sixty years and then reappeared with five young children, four girls and one boy, who all looked extremely sad.

The Green Lady's daughter is said to be buried outside of Florida, under a tree named after her, 'Kay.' The reason of death is marked on the tree.

Molly Duddy (11)
St Anne's Primary School, Rosemount, Co Londonderry

The Life Of Kenny Dalglish

Although I wasn't born in the 1970s, a person I greatly admire is the past Liverpool and Celtic player, Kenny Dalglish.

Kenny was born on the 4th March 1951 in the city of Glasgow in Scotland. He won a total of 102 caps for Scotland and he played for Celtic from 1970 until 1977, scoring a record of 112 goals. He then went to play for Liverpool and quickly became a favourite of the fans. During his thirteen years with them, they won the Championship nine times.

After he left Liverpool, he stopped playing and started his managing career. His team to manage was the unimpressive Blackburn Rovers, and surprised everyone by taking them from the bottom to the top of the league. This he did in his first season with the once unimpressive team! He went on to lead them to win the Championship in 1995, their first since 1914.

After leaving Blackburn, the team fell straight back to the bottom of the league.

In 1996, he became manager of Newcastle United, again proving his skill. He led them to the FA Cup final in his second season. He left in 1998 and is now a director with Celtic.

Darragh Coyle (11)
St Anne's Primary School, Rosemount, Co Londonderry

HEADLESS HORSEMAN

One dark night, John and Bob, two friends, were walking down the streets of Brandywell in Derry at 10:30pm when they heard some strange noises, like a horse and cart. Bob thought, who would be coming down the lane at this time of night? They saw the Headless Horseman. They ran as fast as their feet would take them. John tripped over his laces and the Horseman ran him over and broke his back. Bob ran and got away.

The Horseman is a very popular ghost story in Derry. Many people in Derry tell ghost stories when they are having fun, maybe in the street.

A Headless Horseman ruled some people for many years, but was then killed in Cork in 1965. Then in 1974, he rose from the dead. Some people don't believe in him, but others do.

Jonathan Patton (11)
St Anne's Primary School, Rosemount, Co Londonderry

A STRANGE HAPPENING

It all began when five teenage boys set out to camp overnight. That night, they sat around a fire and set dares. One dare was that at midnight, they would go to a house which was said to be haunted. Midnight approached, so they set off for the house. The house was only about a mile away from where they were camping.

As they approached the dark gate of the house, shivers went up their backs as bats soared above them. Still shaking, they entered through the gate. When they reached the top of the steps, the door opened slightly. They entered the house, still shaking. As they walked around the house, a dark shadow followed them but the boys didn't notice anything. Before they knew it, the five of them were in a dark room with only each other and the unknown person. After that, nobody heard of them again. What happened? Nobody knows.

Nicole Keenan (11)
St Anne's Primary School, Rosemount, Co Londonderry

WHEN THE LORD FOUND THE MOBILE

It was a summer's day and the rain had just stopped when my granda came in and said, 'Molly, Laura, today we're going up the mountain to find my mobile.' So we got in the car.

Hours and hours went past with no sign of the mountain, then we pulled up at the big mucky place. 'OK,' he said.
I asked, 'Why did we stop here?'
He said, 'We're here.'

I said to Molly, 'What kind of place is this?'
We started to walk up the hill when my foot got stuck in mud. It pulled off my shoe. I shouted,
'Granda! My shoe came off!'

The my granda said, 'I'm ringing the phone.' Then I heard a little tune. I pulled my shoe right out and saw the mobile. I held it up and announced
 I had found it.
Then my granda shouted, 'The Lord found the mobile!'
In a quiet voice I said, 'I found the mobile.'

Laura Duddy (11)
St Anne's Primary School, Rosemount, Co Londonderry

MY FRIENDS

My friends are really nice. My best friend is Hayley McMullan. I met her in P1 and she said, 'Will you be my friend?' My other friends are Laura, Meghan, Soraya, Michaela and many, many more. Laura is my friend. She takes care of me when I'm sick or hurt.

My friends from the street are Regina, Jessica, Claire and some other people. Regina is my other best friend, we go to parties together and everywhere together, even the same school. Jessica is my other best friend. She is in the same school as me, but in P4. Regina is in P6.

All my friends are the best.

Bronagh McGinley (11)
St Anne's Primary School, Rosemount, Co Londonderry

ONE PUPPY TOO MANY

When Billy was going to bed on Saturday night, his dad told him something exciting. He said that his dog called Pebbles would have her puppies during the night. Dad made a bed for her in the shed. Billy took her some food and water. He locked the door, said goodnight and went up to his bed. He tried to sleep, but he was too excited and he just could not wait until morning.

There was Pebbles and her puppies. He counted them, there were seven. Two black ones, a brown one, two little white ones. Billy just loved them all and he took good care of them when they were growing up. His favourite was the tiniest white one. She was the last to do everything, but she got there in the end.

The puppies stayed with their mummy for six weeks, but then they had to go to their new homes. Billy felt very sad as one by one the puppies went with their new owners. He had to be very brave when they left. He knew the day would come when Polly, the tiny white one, would go too. He begged his dad to let him keep her, but his dad said, 'Two dogs are too many!' Billy begged and begged his dad, and then he caved in. Billy was so happy!

Jade Healy (11)
St Anne's Primary School, Rosemount, Co Londonderry

KILLER IN THE BACK SEAT!

A woman went to a bar with a couple of friends and stayed there until the early hours of the morning. After, she went to her car then saw the car had no petrol. She went to a nearby petrol station. When the man went to fill up the car with petrol, he looked in, and he thought he saw someone. He went inside the petrol station shop, came out minutes later and said 'There is someone who wants to talk to you.' So she went to the phone and no one was on the line. the man closed the door and said, 'There's someone and . . .' Before he could finish, she pushed the man and ran out to the car and went. As the man got to his feet, he shouted, 'There's someone in the back seat!' But the woman couldn't hear him and kept on driving. When she was driving, a man/woman came out from the back seat with an axe. Then the window broke and the woman's head came out with the axe.

Always check the back seat!

Ryan Curran (11)
St Anne's Primary School, Rosemount, Co Londonderry

CHLOE'S BIG MISTAKE

'Chloe, wake up. Time for school!' shouted a very familiar voice.
'Mmmm, can't. Too tired!' was the very enthusiastic answer.
Then comes her sister with a jug of water. 'Get up Chloe, you have to take me to school *now,* or Miss Sweeney will be so cross!' that was her little sister Jessica, pining to get to the P2 magic teacher. They called her that because the P2s all love her and that's not normal!

Chloe screamed, 'Arghhh! There's water all over my bed. Jessica, I'm going to kill you!'
'Aha! Twinkle says you can't because I'm so cute!'
Chloe was in the bathroom thinking of an evil plan for revenge. Then finally, it hit her!

What did Jessica love the most in the world? Her pet rabbit, Twinkle! Chloe let Twinkle out, but Twinkle accidentally escaped. Chloe felt awful. She had only wanted to make Jessica nervous, but now Twinkle really had escaped. Jessica's eyes were streaming. Chloe was feeling so bad, that she got Jessica a new rabbit. She had well and truly learnt her lesson. Revenge isn't always sweet.

Leona Gillen (11)
St Anne's Primary School, Rosemount, Co Londonderry

THE DAY I SAW ARSENAL

It was a cold Saturday morning and me and my daddy had arrived at Luton Airport in England. We got the train to London and walked around for a while in Oxford Street. I got a new game in Virgin.

At 2:30pm we headed off to Arsenal's stadium. We got to our seats which were over at the side of the North Bank at 3:00pm. This is the story of that match.

5 minutes: Van Bronckhorst runs down the wing, crosses low into the box, Lauren is there, it's a goal!

7 minutes: Brevett crosses into the box for Marlet who heads towards goal . . . it's in! 1-1.

21 minutes: Lauren has the ball on the right wing, he gives the ball to Vieira who hits it first time! Goal! 2-1 to Arsenal!

32 minutes: Vieira gives the ball to him and Henry slips the ball past Van Der Sar! 3-1! Is it over?

67 minutes: Lauren crosses low into the box, Fulham can't get it out, Henry uses his knee to put it in! It's over! 4-1!

And that's how it ended.

Niall Conwell (11)
St Anne's Primary School, Rosemount, Co Londonderry

RACE TO THE TOP!

A young girl called Amy was entered in a talent contest. There were five contestants, one of which was a girl called Chloe. Both girls were cousins and both had great voices. One of them was expected to win. Everyone was betting one of the two would win!

On the night, both were great. When the voting started, the lead changed three times in the first half hour. In the last ten minutes, the vote took another turn, family members had a tough choice! Then the voting stopped. Who had won?

The results were read out. In second place were Chloe and Amy. Everybody was shocked! First place went to Anna Sweeny. Silence flooded the room, nobody could believe it. A recount was ordered, but Anna still won. She got her medal and everybody cheered.

Catherine Duffy (11)
St Anne's Primary School, Rosemount, Co Londonderry

A DREAM DAY

One day me, my daddy and my mummy and brother decided to go for a day out because there was no work, no school and it was a beautiful day. On the way to the park where we decided to go, me and my brother wished we could go to Disneyland instead. We stopped off at a shop to get some things for the picnic.

Soon the journey was over and we were at the park. My brother and I played for a while. Everyone felt hungry, so we decided to have our picnic. When I was eating my crisps, I felt something hard in my mouth, so I spat it out. When I spat it out, I saw that it was a golden nugget. On the crisp packet, it said if you find a golden nugget, then four people will win a trip to Disneyland.

I told my brother and my mummy and daddy. We were all excited. My daddy drove like a madman back to the shop to see if it was real and on the way, we bumped into another car. Suddenly I woke up realising it was all a dream!

Maria Grumley (11)
St Anne's Primary School, Rosemount, Co Londonderry

THE HAUNTED HOUSE

It grabbed my shoulder. I was doomed . . .

I rushed inside, out of the nipping rain. It was one of the unlucky days when the rain pours and you happen not to have a coat. I stepped into the old house to find it was humid, the exact climate of a rainforest. I cried out to see if anyone was there. There was a quiet creak as something emerged down the long and never-ending stairs. I backed against the wall. I stayed paralysed as I waited, half-scared to death. From the stairs, a black creature emerged slowly from the black shade. It was a cat with a look of hunger. I tried to attract it with my tuna sandwich, but it stared at me constantly. I ran as the cat pounced on me. It turned into a big bear. I ran away, up the never-ending stairs. When I got to the top, a furry hand came on top of mine. It grabbed my shoulder. I was doomed . . .

'She's done it again! That rascal Goldilocks! The last porridge. It's gone,' raged Father Bear.

Kyung-Won Yoon (10)
St Bride's Primary School, Belfast, Co Antrim

A DAY IN THE LIFE OF A BOOK

I lay on the table, sore and tired. She'd picked me up and put me down nearly every five minutes. I'd had enough already. Her baby brother had got into the bathroom last night and stuck me down the toilet. Now think how you'd feel if someone did it to you. My pages have been wrinkled and changed colour, from pure white to a dirty yellow. I hate it, but worst of all, I dreaded the boy. You can still read me, but she was that busy doing little jobs for her parents, I felt as though she wasn't interested in me. She used to never be able to put me down and I know manners come first, but this is crazy, she didn't even make a big deal when I was stuffed down the toilet and now I feel rejected.

Hannah McGrath (11)
St Bride's Primary School, Belfast, Co Antrim

A GHOSTLY EXPERIENCE

It was a dull, rainy day. The wind was howling. Normally this is how Katie liked it, but today was different, she had plans with her friend Lucy, but the rain was too heavy to go outside! She decided to explore her new house, an old Victorian one . . .

She searched for the attic; she thought it would be the best place to look. When she got there, she discovered a little surprise.
'Arghhh!' she screamed, petrified as she spotted the ghost. 'What are you doing here?'
'I have lived here for 100 years, please help me,' returned a wheezy voice.
'I'll do what I can,' said Katie, and the ghost told her just what to do!

The next day the weather had cleared up and Katie went up to the attic to find the ghost. When she found him, she tried to remember everything she knew about history, she was an A student, you see. This ghost was lost in time and he had forgotten what year he was supposed to be in, so he had asked Katie to help him remember!

After a while, he remembered where he was from. 'Thank you, Katie!' And the ghost was off!

Catherine Loughrey (11)
St Bride's Primary School, Belfast, Co Antrim

TOMB RAIDER

I am a tomb raider. I have to be ready for the real thing, so I go training and have to get through the made-up tomb, which is just as hard and complicated as the real one. OK, I enter the tomb first, I see holes in the wall and I get a piece of paper and an arrow shoots right through it. I say to myself, I'm glad I wasn't there. Now there was a big, vicious dog. I quickly pulled out my handgun and shot it. Next, a narrow way with a big hole. I could jump that, no problem. Come on, this is too easy. I jumped, it began to get wider, I got to it but only just. I was hanging on with my fingers. A low arrow shot across, grazing my fingers painfully. I pulled myself up and I saw the button. I went up and pushed it, I'd done it!

Andrew Gribben (10)
St Bride's Primary School, Belfast, Co Antrim

THE RAINBOW

The sky looked a bit green today. Ever since Mars exploded and crashed into Pluto, we've been having all the colours of the rainbow. Dad's a bit annoyed at this because as he's a shepherd, he's always predicting the weather. You know the old saying, 'Red sky at night, shepherd's delight.' It's really half his job you see, because he gets money if he's right about the weather. Anyway, let's got on with the story.

One night when I was lying in bed, I looked out of the window and saw a huge, bright red ball coming straight for my house! I only found out later that what I had seen was really the remains of Mars. I quickly woke my dad up and got him to look out of the window.
'Oh my gosh!' he cried, 'we've got to stop it immediately!'
He ran outside, only in his underwear, screaming at me to get his shrink ray. (He's also an inventor.) I ran to the basement and grabbed a strange green machine labelled *Shrink Ray*. I ran back outside with it. As soon as he got it, he pressed a multicoloured button and . . . the ball shrank to the dize of a pea! *Yippee!*

Hannah Smyth (11)
St Bride's Primary School, Belfast, Co Antrim

THE MURDER HOUSE

In our new house I felt very uncomfortable, and it felt very haunted. Every night, you could hear a blood-curdling scream, well at least I heard it, but when I asked anyone else, they said, 'I heard nothing.' I was getting really scared because the scream sounded like it was getting nearer and my mum and dad wouldn't let me go up to the attic, because that was where the screaming was coming from. I was getting restless, I had to go up, I just had to, so one night I secretly went into the attic. It was easy because the attic door was next to mine. So I went up, but there was nothing there except a fake skeleton, although I thought it was false. Suddenly I heard footsteps coming up the stairs so I went and hid behind this big wardrobe, the only other thing in the attic. But the person who came in was not my mum or dad, it was a servant lady. Then the master came in and took out a knife and killed her. Don't ask why, because next I saw his mad eyes coming as he brought the knife down . . .

Jessica Rusk (11)
St Bride's Primary School, Belfast, Co Antrim

THE GHOST STORY OF CASTLEWELLAN FOREST PARK

We were at Castlewellan Forest Park on a Hallowe'en night. All of us were with the camp leaders and had a lot of fun coming down on the coach. Everyone put up their tents and decorated them.

Orla toasted marshmallows over the fire, our leader, Gary, fell asleep so we played games. Suddenly, I heard an eerie sound coming from the trees, I thought it was only the rattling of the tree branches. Then another creaking sound, we got worried, saying it was twelve o'clock. Then suddenly, a ghost appeared, it was so scary, and said in a eerie voice, 'Survive until 3am, then you will still be alive every day.' He then told us that after 3am, a ghost would take you over if you fell asleep, then you would become a ghost.

After hearing this, we all tried to stay up. Stephanie nearly fell asleep, the others nudged her. We drank coffee, and more coffee, the ghosts were surrounding us, singing lullabies. We were so tempted to fall asleep. Jessica tried to hit a ghost, but her hand went through it.

Then it struck me, I remembered my CD player and I put on 'Grease.' We all got up and started dancing. It was past 4am and the ghosts were still there . . . they were dancing too!

Maria Chesser (11)
St Bride's Primary School, Belfast, Co Antrim

THE DESERTED HOUSE

It all started one rainy and miserable-looking morning during my summer break - except it didn't look much like summer to me - but anyway, as I was saying, it *was* summer and we'd rented a cottage by a lake. I walked down to the lake because I was bored. I was skimming stones across the water, when I noticed a strange-looking girl by the bank. She was wet and was wearing weird clothes. As she approached she said, 'Hello, my name's Beth. What's yours?'

'Katherine,' I said.

'Do you want to play hide-and-seek in that house?'

'Okay.'

When it was my turn to hide, I went into a room with no furniture, only an old newspaper lying on the ground. It was dated 19th July 1902.

That's one hundred years ago today! A headline caught my eye. *Tragedy At Lake.* I thought it sounded interesting, so I read on. *'The body of eleven-year-old Beth Williams was recovered from the Black Lake today. It seems Beth was playing by the river when she slipped and fell in.'*

A shiver ran up my spine and my body tingled all over. It couldn't be! Could it?

Katherine McCann (11)
St Bride's Primary School, Belfast, Co Antrim

A DAY IN THE LIFE OF A FIVE POUND NOTE

Today was probably going to be another ordinary day. Yes, another day in the dark and gloomy purse. I was the only five pound note in the purse and I was too scared to make friends with the ten pound notes, or the twenty, because they were much bigger than me. Then the woman opened her purse and took me out, I was so glad to see the light. The shopkeeper took hold of me, opened the till and put me in. It was fantastic. All the other five pound notes welcomed me. We chatted about how good it is to be a five pound note. We had a great time until something dreadful happened. The shopkeeper opened the till and took me out. I was so scared. What was she going to do to me? Then I realised that another woman needed change. She had spent fifteen pounds. The woman had given the shopkeeper twenty, so she needed five pounds change. I was given to the woman and went into the purse. Luckily, there was another five pound note. We became best friends. I was so happy. This purse was exactly the same as the other, so there was no change!

Stephanie Prince (11)
St Bride's Primary School, Belfast, Co Antrim

A Day In The Life Of A Pound Coin

It is morning at last. I am in the back pocket of some person's jeans, waiting to be spent. I am a pound coin and am thrown around. I have no friends or family and am all alone.

At last the jeans are being put on, I now have a chance of being spent. My owner has taken me from the pocket and is holding me tightly in her palm. Her hands are all sweaty and damp and I am becoming terribly wet. She is walking to a shop and is trading me for a Mars Bar and a packet of Skittles.

I am in a till. It is dark and small and I am lying wondering whose hands I shall lie in next. The till is being opened and all of us coins are lying anxiously and hopeful to be taken out. Our hearts are let down, only a five pound note has been pulled out, and a ten pound note has been put in, in exchange. All of us coins are left again in the dark. This is my home for tonight.

Maria Cushinan (11)
St Bride's Primary School, Belfast, Co Antrim

THE HOUSE ON HAUNTED HILL

Last Hallowe'en, my friends and I didn't trick or treat. When I went to the shop to get sweets for the trick or treaters, I was told that I was the one millionth customer. The owner told my friends and I to come to a Hallowe'en party. We agreed to go. After the owner gave us the directions, he said that there was one catch, he told us that some people said that the house wass haunted.

When we got there, we noticed that we were the only people not wearing costumes, well, apart from the man that owned the shop. We were slightly embarrassed so we went over to him to talk to him. He was standing in front of a strange grandfather clock. The clock struck twelve, hairs started coming out of the man. We took a few steps back. He was a werewolf! Two vampires said, 'You simply have to join us for dinner.'
I replied, 'It's okay, we're full.'
Then the creatures started moving towards us, a vampire spoke again, she said, 'I don't think you understand. You are dinner!'

As she was speaking I woke up, it was just a nightmare.

Luke McCann
St Bride's Primary School, Belfast, Co Antrim

A Day In The Life Of A . . .

I'm taken out of my bag and put into a dark room. It's plastic and hard.
I'm put in with an apple and two chocolate bars, plus a drink. Later that
day, I'm taken out and looked at. My owner is joking and talking. She is
small and has brown hair. I'm put back and the two chocolate bars are
eaten. Soon, it's lunch and I'm taken, opened, crunched and emptied.
My wrapper is put in the plastic lunchbox. After a bumpy ride, I'm put
in a bin and make loads of friends. It's the end of my day. Can you
guess what I am?

A packet of crisps.

Stephanie Ferguson (11)
St Bride's Primary School, Belfast, Co Antrim

A Glorious Victory

The day has come when I must swallow my fears, I must keep control of my nerves. I can hear the crowd shouting and squealing with all their might, their voices are full of excitement, our manager is telling us to hurry up. He walks away, I keep watching him. I see him pay our coach bundles of money. Our coach walks into the middle of us, the football players, and he tells us to sit on the benches and he starts to tell us moves and skills to do.

A garda walks into the changing rooms and says, 'Let's get this match on the road.' There is a garda for each player. We step out into the tunnel, the crowds are yelling our team's name. I get a strong smell, I look into the crowd, there's tons of people smoking. It doesn't smell nice. I get a strong taste of vinegar, it is coming off chips. I wait nervously and then I run out onto the pitch, tapping the fans' hands as I go.

James Donnelly (11)
St Dympna's Primary School, Dromore, Co Tyrone

A Day In The Life Of Michael Owen

I'm in the dressing room, I'm putting on my boots and I'm so afraid and scared. The manager shouts at us, he says, 'You have come this far, don't let me down. Come on boys, good luck and get on. Don't be long, they'll be ready for you in 20 minutes. It is so warm in here. Time is up boys, come on.'

We are out on the pitch. The crowd is shouting at us, the national anthem comes first and then the game starts. The referee blows the whistle and the game begins.

Roisin McAleer (11)
St Dympna's Primary School, Dromore, Co Tyrone

A Day In The Life Of Roy Keane

I am playing in the Word Cup Final. I am quite nervous, but our manager is trying to calm us down. I am lying on the bench and the doctor is rubbing my legs to try and settle me before going out to play the match. Now I am going to get my jersey on. I can hear a faint roar from the crowd. I am putting my boots on, we are getting up to go out now.

We are in the tunnel, some of us are still shaking, but most of us are OK, well not too bad, anyway! I can smell the smell of chips, vinegar and some hot dogs. People are shouting and roaring for us to hurry up and get the game started. I am holding on as tight as I can to the rails. We all have to do some stretches. More people are shouting for us to come out, and we are on our way out.

Louise Slevin (10)
St Dympna's Primary School, Dromore, Co Tyrone

THE BEST PRESENT EVER

The best present I have ever received was when my baby brother Oran was born. All the anticipation was intense. I was very nervous, but when he was born on the 24th March, he was a beautiful baby. He had no hair at first. All my worry was over and I was really happy. I just hoped that he would be all right and healthy throughout life and he would stay as lovely as he was then.

Oran was very small and tiny, but then as he grew older, he got bigger. I was worried at first because Mum had to go into hospital for at least three days, but as the days went on, I started to get very anxious. But when he was born, I wasn't worried anymore. This was my best and favourite present, all I could ever ask for. I was delighted.

Cara Sludden (11)
St Dympna's Primary School, Dromore, Co Tyrone

A Day In The Life Of Keano

I am in the dressing room. It is the World Cup Final, Ireland v Brazil. Twenty minutes to kick-off and I am extremely nervous. Mick has told me I am playing in the centre of defensive midfield. He has given me the captain's armband, so I feel very honoured. Mick is giving us some last minute tactics. I am marking Rivaldo. Right now, I am tying my boots and getting ready to walk out the tunnel.

We are now in the tunnel shaking hands with each other. I am shaking hands with Rivaldo, he is very friendly. I can hear the crowd waiting anxiously with loud cheers and roars. The referee is calling us out. The crowd are cheering wildly. There are balloons, banners, flags, toilet rolls, air horns and flares everywhere. The colours and noises are vivid. Every player on the pitch is sweating with nervousness. I picked up a blade of grass and blessed myself with it. The referee called me and the other captain over. I won the toss. Suddenly, the whistle blew and the crowd roared wildly. This is a dream come true.

Ruairí McNulty (10)
St Dympna's Primary School, Dromore, Co Tyrone

ENTERING THE STADIUM!

I'm in the dressing rooms with my mates. We're tightening our boots. In half an hour, the kick-off will start. I'm jumping, but I'll be OK after I get on the pitch. I can hear referees in the tunnel who'll watch and who will be on the field. I can hear the manager roaring, 'Don't let me down, boys!'

I'm going through the tunnel, I'm nervous. I can smell sausages and chips. I'm taking centre today on the pitch. I am standing beside Manchester United, and Roy Keane is taking centre also. I can hear cheers for me and my mates. My best mate is in goal. 'We'll win!' everyone shouts at us. I have met the referee and shaken hands with him, he seems very nice. There are a couple of rough players on the pitch. I can see the pitch from here, I'm very nervous to get playing in the field. We're on the pitch, the referee calls, 'Kick-off!'

Edel Goulding (11)
St Dympna's Primary School, Dromore, Co Tyrone

A Day In The Life Of Shay Given

I'm sitting in the dressing room tightening my studs and laces, pulling my jersey over my head. The tension is rising in the dressing room. The physio is making me do stretches in case I get another groin strain like a did a fortnight before. (My manager is saying how proud he is and telling us the tactics.) We can hear the referee of the World Cup Final, from Ukraine, talking to his assistants from Korea and France. The teams are anxious. We are getting up out of our seats, the manager in his £2,000 suit telling us to get up.

We come out to the tunnel. The other team is already there. We all shake hands with our opponents, Portugal. I am throwing the ball against the wall. The atmosphere is electric. I can taste the hot dogs and chips. I smell the sweat of the players, the noise is rising more than ever. I see the short, green grass, a section of the fans and the goalposts. I pass the ball to the huge defender. I pat the best midfielder, for me anyway. The referee leads us out to an electric atmosphere.

Ryan McDermott (10)
St Dympna's Primary School, Dromore, Co Tyrone

THE STADIUM!

I'm sitting here in the dressing rooms. My heart is pounding. The coach is going on at the goalie saying, 'Don't you dare let one goal in!' and I'm pretty sure he's going to move on to us next. Oh look, there's Tom coming up the middle of the room with the jerseys. My number is lucky seven. Our jerseys are red and white. I'm putting on my jersey, the other players are doing their stretches, but John the goalie, is too nervous to do anything. We eventually manage to calm him down. Five minutes to go now!

I can see teddies dressed in our strip being thrown on to the field. I can also see the band playing a very catchy tune. I can smell the hot dogs and popcorn. I didn't touch anything, but I did shake hands with the opponents. I could taste the sweat in my mouth as it ran down my face. I step out of the tunnel and the crowd roars. Suddenly, all my fears disappear!

Ashlene McDonnell (11)
St Dympna's Primary School, Dromore, Co Tyrone

WHITE LIGHTNING!

I am on a horse galloping at break-neck speed. A jump nears, we go flying over it. Nothing can stop us. A crack of the whip, faster, faster. Zooming through the fields of lush green grass, I feel the wind twisting round my hair. I feel the horse's blood pulsing rapidly as we bolt past. I can hear the birds rising as we gallop.

My horse is dapple-grey and white. Her name is White Lightning because she's as fast as the wind and quick as lightning. The world around becomes a blur. Faster, faster we go, practically flying at our speed. All I smell is dust and dirt she kicks up from the ground. It starts to rain, but that doesn't stop us. Over a hedge we jump. Rain thunders down on us. We are slowing, slowing and stopping. I jump off and tend to my exhausted horse. 'Well done, we won!'

Paula Teague (11)
St Dympna's Primary School, Dromore, Co Tyrone

ENTERING THE STADIUM

I'm tightening my bootlaces and tying my shorts up. I'm putting on my jersey, I'm number nine. Our manager is telling us our tactics, he's telling the keeper to kick the ball to the wings. I'm putting on my shin guards. The players are fidgeting with their fingers. They're muttering to themselves, saying their prayers to God, asking him to look after them if they get badly injured on the pitch. I feel nervous to be playing a final game. I have the world watching me play a game for my team. I can hear cheering sounds in the air, whistling and aerosol cans and the rippling sounds from the flags.

Walking down the tunnel, I can smell the grease of the food. I can taste the vinegar on the chips in the air. I can see men in orange jackets at the end of the tunnel, they look like flames. The manager hands the ball to me. The smooth leather on the ball gives me a good feeling. We might just win!

Patrick Irvine (11)
St Dympna's Primary School, Dromore, Co Tyrone

THE MIDNIGHT HORSES

It all began on New Year's day. I went for a long walk on my own. Suddenly, I heard a noise, but I couldn't recognise what it was. Scared out of my wits, I ran to the nearest house but before I got to knock on the door, it opened by itself.

As I was walking down the long, dark corridor, I heard screaming and crying noises. I walked on into the living room to find an old man tied to a bloody chair. When I untied him, I asked him if he knew what the noises where that I had heard outside. He said they were the midnight horses. I asked what they were and this is what he said:

'The midnight horses first came 100 years ago. They belonged to an Irish farmer. On this date, 100 years ago, the farmer's daughter was kidnapped, so at midnight on the first of January every year, the midnight horses go looking for her. Do you know who the little girl is? It's *you*!'

Laura Molloy (11)
St John's Primary School, Middletown, Co Armagh

THE TIME PORTAL

It all began when I was messing with my real robot's parts. I put a part in the wrong place and it opened a time portal. I was very afraid so I closed it and left it for a day. Then I went to a fortune teller in Armagh and he said, 'You will change the future.' I went home wondering what that meant and asked myself if this was true.

Today was Friday the 13th and I was going into the time portal. My voyage back through time was very rough, but I got there in one piece. I realised that I was in the dino age. I found out that dinosaurs were tame and not bloodthirsty. I was still living until 2000. I saved them from extinction. Now in the year 2002, dinosaurs still live.

John-James Hughes (11)
St John's Primary School, Middletown, Co Armagh

FIRST DAY

For the first time in my life, I didn't want to leave the car. People were actually trying to prise me out of my seat. I felt like a dog, now I know how Bridie felt. I was mostly scared of a strange woman called Mrs Kelly, but although she said it a million times, I still think she wanted to eat me.

'Finally, now it's time to meet your new classmates. Let me tell you, you're going to have super fun!' cried Miss O'Connor, my new teacher, after having a whispered talk with my mum. We started off painting and I painted a bunny with a carrot next to it. We had a break, where I got to know everyone else. I learned how to count to five. 'One, two, three, four, five.' Then we played hairdressers with real scissors, but the teacher told us off.

'Well,' began my mum, 'did you have an eventful day?'
'Oh yes,' I exclaimed, 'and you said it would be awful!'

Colette Hughes (11)
St John's Primary School, Middletown, Co Armagh

WATCH YOUR STEP

What I am about to tell you will shock you to your very core. One night, my friend Chris and I were taking a stroll on the beach, when suddenly he fainted. I picked him up easily because he wasn't heavy or tall. I noticed a cut on the sole of his foot, but it wasn't a normal cut. The cut was bordered by pea-green fluid. Putting him down gently, I headed for the phone box and called 999. By the time the ambulance found us, Chris had died. They brought him to the morgue for a post-mortem, but he wasn't there for long. The doctor explained to the police that the skin of the body had jumped off the skeleton and out of the window!

Legend has it that every year since, on the date he died, he sucks the soul out of another person. Chris died fifty years ago today, and it is said the he will kill me, my family and everyone who knows this tale.

Declan McBride (11)
St John's Primary School, Middletown, Co Armagh

THE SURPRISE FIND

Hi, my name is Cormac. I'm an archaeologist from Ireland. This is the story of how I found a leprechaun.

One day, me and my companions found a cave. We went in to explore. It was as dark as night. We got out our torches to look around. I heard something, but we walked on. Soon, all of us were hearing strange noises. We thought we were surrounded, so we stood still. I turned my head and saw a leprechaun! I don't know what came over me because before I knew it, I was running after it. I ran and ran. Then I dived and caught it. I ran back to my companions who were wondering where I was. I showed them the leprechaun. Then, we heard another noise so we ran out.

It was now night. I looked to see what time it was and the leprechaun escaped. We ran after it. It was trying to put a spell on us. We chased it down a hole which we filled up with anything we could find.

If you ever go to Cork and hear a strange noise, you might just know what it is!

Cormac Long (11)
St John's Primary School, Middletown, Co Armagh

A Day In The Life Of Squeak

It's Tuesday morning and I am awake in my bed of hay. Bubble was awake before me. When I got out of my bed, I went on the treadmill and waited on Sid to come and feed me. I was feeling very hungry waiting. He was really long, so I gnawed on the bars and it woke him up. I am small, with lots of fur. I have blue eyes and oh, there's little claws Bubble! Hello Bubble! I am introducing myself. Now, where was I? My colour is brindle and I have a long tail, just about three millimetres longer than Bubble's. I am just going to go over to the cardboard tubes, to Bubble.

After lunch, when the children were at school, Mrs Sparrow gave us away to two little boys. The little boys' mummy saw the little boys with us, grabbed us off them, stormed up the path and gave us back to Mrs Sparrow.

It is teatime and Mrs Sparrow has set Bubble and me on a big, high thing. In a few minutes a strong man lifted us and brought us to Mrs Sparrow. He said, 'You cannot put this in the bin because there are living creatures in here!'

Mrs Sparrow brought us back in. Sid and Amy lifted us out of the cage. Amy put me up Sid's trouser leg. I was wondering what was happening. I got tired at seven o'clock, so Sid put me to bed - just before he went.

Melissa McComb (8)
St Mary's Primary School, Killyleagh, Co Down

A Day In The Life Of Squeak

It is Tuesday morning and I'm awake in my cage. I looked out of the bars, but there was nobody there. I am the first one awake again! Bubble, who is fast asleep, lies peacefully in the straw, so I get to my feet to do some exercise. I ran through my small tunnel and went on the treadmill. After that, I felt quite hungry and puffed out.

My name is Squeak. I have bright brindle fur and eyes as small as beads.

Later that morning, I found myself at a different place - some place where I've never been before. I was in another house and my cage was sitting on the window sill. Over the window were some bright red curtains. I walked over to the bars, pushed my head through and gnawed at them for a few minutes, until I heard someone coming down the stairs. Then all I heard was a very loud scream. There, standing at the door behind me, was a woman looking terrified and for some reason, she was looking at me. As she ran away again, she went upstairs. I heard a lot of shouting and screaming, then a lot of people thudding downstairs. At first they all looked at me! Then Sid lifted my cage and went into the kitchen where everyone got their breakfast. Mrs Sparrow set me on the dustbin and a few minutes later, I was carried to the door by two strong arms. The arms handed me over to Mrs Sparrow and she shut the door quickly. When the children came back from school, they played with me. After their tea, Sid fed me and put me in my cage. I ate my food and went for a long, peaceful nap.

Caoimhe Gordon (9)
St Mary's Primary School, Killyleagh, Co Down

A DAY IN THE LIFE OF BUBBLE

It is Monday morning. I'm awake in my cage and I think it is six o'clock. I am gnawing on the bars of the cage and I'm feeling hungry. Then Squeak woke up and he started running in his wheel.

My name is Bubble, I'm a gerbil. A boy named Sid took us home with him and put us in the larder, but we were caught because his mum heard me gnawing on the bars of the cage. Now Mrs Sparrow hates us and Bill is not very happy to have us around the house. That's about it so far.

At last, Sid has woken up. It's seven o'clock. He has to get ready for school and so does Peggy. Amy is in bed asleep. She doesn't have to get ready for school because she is too young yet. So Sid puts some food and water in our cage and walks over to eat his breakfast. Peggy came and petted me and said, 'Good Bubble.' She always knows me because I have a darker brindle coat than Squeak. I was really hungry by now, so I started eating. I shoved Squeak out of the way so I would get to it first.

After my breakfast, I went on the wheel for about . . . erm . . . an hour. Suddenly, our cage started to shake as Mrs Sparrow lifted it and put it on a big, black bin. It was very high up, but just when the bin was going to be lifted by a very strong man, he took us back to the house and gave us back to Mrs Sparrow. Amy was standing behind her and started crying. So now we are back in the house and we are not going to be given away, because Mrs Sparrow started promising not to give us away because Amy started crying.

Well, it's bedtime now, I'm going to sleep. Wait, 'What's that sound, Squeak?'
'It's Amy crying. She must have had a bad dream.'
'Oh well, today wasn't a very usual day, was it? Goodnight.'

Adam Colgan (9)
St Mary's Primary School, Killyleagh, Co Down

A Day In The Life Of Bubble

Hello, I'm bubble and this morning I woke up on something very high up from the ground, called a dustbin. As I turned to see where I was, I saw a huge thing with wheels on it and it was coming towards me. A man came over and he lifted up the cage towards the house. The nice warm hay that I sleep in shook and bounced while the man was walking. While this was happening, I was the only one in the cage that was awake. All I heard at the door was shouting and yelling. I felt really scared and miserable.

Let me tell you a little about myself. First of all, I'm a gerbil. I am a very dark brindle, I've got a very long tail, I don't like Mrs Sparrow very much, but I like Sid, Peggy, Amy and Bill Sparrow.

Next I was fed by Sid. I like Sid a lot. After a while, I exercised on my wheel for a few minutes. I took a rest for fifteen minutes, then we played about for a while. Sid chased me up and down and around and around the house. When Mrs Sparrow heard all the noise, she came in and shouted at Sid. She ordered Sid to put me back in my cage and put me in the cupboard in his room. When he had done that, she told him to lock the cupboard and give her the key. After that, all I heard was shouting, yelling, screaming and crying. All the noise I heard was giving me a sore head, I felt like it was going to explode.

All the rest of the day was quiet and calm. There was no shouting yelling, screaming or crying. All I heard was the sounds of voices coming from the television. Finally, Mrs Sparrow let Sid bring me out of the cupboard.

At teatime, for once, Mrs Sparrow gave me a treat. She gave me something that was easy to bite. It was nice, cold, that's the way I like my food, and it was lovely and bright. Later on, Squeak asked me what kind of a day I had, because Bill Sparrow had him all day. I said I had a really weird day, and then I told him why.

Everyone in the house, including Squeak, was asleep but not me. In about ten or fifteen minutes, I finally got to sleep. It was a good day and a bad day for me and Mrs Sparrow.

Ryan Fegan (9)
St Mary's Primary School, Killyleagh, Co Down

A Day In The Life Of Bubble

When I wake up in the mornings, I always see Squeak doing exercises and I gnawing at the bars. I wake up under the hay and roll over to get the bits of hay which stick to my fur. I always wake up second, because I am the laziest. Then I do my exercise. I love doing running on the treadmill and climbing the bars. I am feeling hungry, thirsty, and most of all, I am feeling tired - and it's only nine o'clock!

Now, let me tell you about myself. I am Bubble, the youngest gerbil. I am speckled and have green eyes. I have sharp nails and teeth and very good hearing. I love vegetables, which are very nice.

Later, when the dustbin men came, Mrs Sparrow set me on a high object and a big glove came closer to me and Squeak. It took us to the door. Alice didn't have a good smile on her face, she would have been glad if we had gone.

In the afternoon I got some lunch and I took a nice nap. When Sid came home from school, I shot right up from my bed and I was overjoyed. I was really glad Sid was home. I played a game with Sid for an hour. Mrs Sparrow was sick of it. Oh well, it's not my fault! I just played on.

At nine o'clock, Sid was sent to bed. All I did was talk to Squeak, which I thought was kind of fun, finding out what she had got up to today. But she didn't do much at all. Then I told her about Sid playing with me and she murmured, 'That must have been fun.' Then she tutted, 'Oh well.'

I had told her all that happened to me that day. I cuddled up in my hay nest and yawned, and then I fell asleep.

Ryan McGreevy (9)
St Mary's Primary School, Killyleagh, Co Down

A Day In The Life Of Squeak

Ahhh, what a yawn! Oh hello, I can talk, but don't tell Sid! Just you and me know, OK? I am in the Mudds. I just can't wait till Sid comes. Well I can a wee bit, because I get my brekkie and I can wait a wee bit because I can't talk, and I love to talk. Now I have to do my exercises. Roll over, roll back, roll over, roll back. Oh I'm just thinking, I forgot to introduce myself. I'm Squeak. My brother is Bubble, he's still asleep! I think maybe he's waking up now. 'Morning Bubble.'

'Morning Squeak, who are you talking to?'

'My invisible friend.'

'There's no such thing as invisible friends.'

'I know, I'm just pretending.'

'Why?'

'Because I want to!'

'Oh!'

I'd better get back to my exercises. Roll over, roll back, roll over, roll back, now I will do my jumping exercise. Actually, I will finish. I'll just sit and wait till the Mudds get up, or I will wait till Sid comes. So, you really want to see me in action? OK, here I go. 'Reach for the stars, climb every mountain, em, em, I forget, sorry.'

Here's Sid, yippee! I'm just going to go on the treadmill while I wait for him to get my food ready. Here he comes. Mmm, mmm, this is lovely. I've nearly finished. Finished! Dawn Mudd is awake now. Yeah! I now can play with both of them. Oh, and if you're wondering what the time is, it's eleven o'clock in the morning and if you want to know how I know, I heard Sid saying.

I'm now rolling up Sid's trouser leg. He's on the mat with Dawn, watching TV. He let me and Bubble out of the cage. Bubble's up Dawn's leg. I think it's five o'clock in the evening now. I'll be going for a nap, or maybe I should nap on his leg, so I think I'll see you tomorrow. Night, night.

Melissa Kent (9)
St Mary's Primary School, Killyleagh, Co Down

A DAY IN THE LIFE OF SQUEAK

It was a lovely morning. I stretched and gave a long yawn. The sun was shining in my cage. Bubble was deep in the hay nest. I was feeling tired and hungry, so I started doing my exercises. I love spinning on the wheel and climbing the bars.

My name is Squeak because Jimmy Dean's cousin called me that. My fur is spiky and my tail is quite small. My eyes are blue. I roll over and have lots of fun. I play with Bubble, my best friend, my only friend too, but sometimes he isn't up on time to play.

My favourite food is cold boiled cabbage. Mmm, lovely! Sid feeds me it all the time. Usually, Sid lets me out on the table in the living room to let me play, but not today. All you could hear was Mrs Sparrow yapping. He hasn't even fed me yet. Maybe he doesn't like me anymore.

Sid came down dressed in his uniform for school. He fed me my favourite food. He went into the hall, slammed the door and ran down the path for school. I saw him get the bus. I hate it when Sid leaves.

Sid's mum came down with Amy and Peggy and went out to take them to school. Bill Sparrow came down to go to work, but before he did, he took the bottle from the cage and filled it with water. Later in the afternoon, Mrs Sparrow came home early. She lifted our cage and put it on the dustbin. Luckily, the dustbin man knocked the door and gave Mrs Sparrow our cage back. He said, 'You can't put living creatures in a dustbin!'

Sid grabbed us. Mr Sparrow had come through the door and Mrs Sparrow finished talking to the man. She shut the door. She could hear sounds of the children and Mr Sparrow laughing. She slammed the kitchen door and made a cup of tea.

Well, this day has been different to any other day! *Phew!*

Stacy Morrison (8)
St Mary's Primary School, Killyleagh, Co Down

A DAY IN THE LIFE OF BUBBLE

It's Tuesday morning and I've woken up. The house is in darkness. I woke up first, I was feeling hungry. The light was turned on and it was Sid. He fed me in my hay nest.

Feeding time is around 8:00am in the morning, lunch is 2:00pm and dinner is 7:00pm.

After breakfast, for exercise I go on the treadmill and that is my play.

Before I forget, I am Bubble, a darker brindle than Squeak who is my twin. Dawn said I have a longer tail by about three millimetres. I got my name from Sid's favourite food, cold boiled cabbage and potato fried with cold meat.

It was five to four and Squeak and I have been given away to two boys. We have to get a duster over our cage so no one can see us. Alice is being very cruel to us because now we will never see Sid again. I was gnawing at the duster when I felt myself bumping down four steps. That was how I knew I was on the move. I bumped into Squeak in horror. I found myself being put down on something quite hard. When the duster was taken off, I saw two identical boys looking at us. They were wearing green and white hooped Celtic tops. A fat woman came in. she was the mother of the children. She took one look at us and I think she said, 'Get them out of here. They are not nice!' I was lifted up and brought back to the Sparrow/Parker's house. There, I saw Peggy and I got to go up Sid's trousers and tickle him.

It had been a happy and sad day. Sad because I was taken away, but happy because I was back where I belong.

Ryan Williams (9)
St Mary's Primary School, Killyleagh, Co Down

A Day In The Life Of Bubble

I woke up in the small corner of my cage. I was the first one up in the house. I sat and waited for someone else to wake up. I was still feeling very tired and just wanted to go back to sleep again, but then Squeak woke up in his cosy corner.

My name is Bubble. I am a gerbil. I am white with brown patches over my body. I love cabbage best. I am always sleeping in my hay nest in my bedroom. Squeak is my best gerbil friend.

I waited till Sid came to feed me. Finally he did come and had cabbage, my favourite food. I ate it peacefully in my corner. Soon I saw Mrs Sparrow coming in the room and she gave me a dirty look. She walked away into the living room with Mr Sparrow.

After breakfast, I went on my treadmill to exercise myself and ran on it for half an hour or so, then I went in my hay nest in the corner and started to doze. Suddenly, a big bump hit me and these two strong arms lifted me. They set my cage on this high thing and opened the cage door. A long, bony thing scuffled about the cage trying to catch us and Squeak got caught. Then another hand came in trying to catch me. I ran about the cage and scurried about, I thought I was going to die. I got caught. Something sat me down on the ground. It was Amy, she was trying to play with me. I ran through a long, dark tube, it was good fun. Then I ran round in circles and was having lots of fun, but just then Mrs Sparrow came walking in. I scuffled over to Squeak and said, 'Squeak, what's going to happen to us?'
Mrs Sparrow said, 'Get them in their cage.'

After that, Sid and Amy went off to school. A knock came on the door, it was two boys. Mrs Sparrow came and we rushed about in the cage. She gave the cage to the boys with us inside. They set off down the street, I bumped my head on the wires. 'Stupid kid!' I said to Squeak.
Squeak replied, 'I know, but where is he taking us?
I replied, 'I think they are taking us away.'

They brought us down a path. Across the road, I saw Sid and Amy. I squeaked and muttered, 'Sid!', but unfortunately Sid didn't hear or see me.

The two boys took us back down the same path. When we got to the Sparrow's house, Mrs Sparrow opened the door. The boys' mother gave us to her. She told Mrs Sparrow, 'We are not having these because we've had them before and they bred! We don't want that to happen again!'

Alice took us back indoors and sat us on the table. She walked off. Amy and Sid took us back out. Sid sat us down on the ground and gave us food. They started to play with us. I climbed up Sid's sleeve to welcome him. He hugged me and put me and Squeak back in the cage before he went to bed. In the cage I talked to Squeak. I said, 'What a day!'
He replied, 'I know, my head is about to fall off!'
'Yes,' I answered, 'that old cow Alice wants to get rid of us, I know she wants to.'
'But if she was so desperate to get rid of us, why not just say so?'
'I don't know. Well for now, let's go off to sleep. It's been a busy day.'

Patrick Bennett (9)
St Mary's Primary School, Killyleagh, Co Down

THE BLUE LADY

A blue lady has been haunting our castle for hundreds of years. No one knows where she is buried, but she will not rest. Some say she was murdered, but no one is really sure of the truth. Her ghost walks the halls and corridors of the castle near where I live. If you are walking past there late at night, you might catch a glimpse of the lady by the window.

Maybe she is watching or waiting for someone who never comes. Whatever she is watching for, she will not be able to rest until it arrives.

Ben Colgan (8)
St Mary's Primary School, Killyleagh, Co Down

ESCAPE TO WITCH MOUNTAIN

Once upon a time there were two babies at the back of a shop. The babies were special, they were born with magic powers. They could make things happen by using their minds. The owner came to see what the purple thing in the sky was, then one minute later, she fainted.

Five years later, the babies were split up. The girl was sent to the children's home. Shortly after, the boy was sent too. When the girl saw the boy, she could not believe her eyes that she had seen her brother again, so while they were in the children's home they went everywhere together, until one day they were being taken away by some rich man. When they arrived, they were amazed when they saw his house. Then two or three days later, the man asked the girl if he could have her magic.

Meanwhile, the girl and the boy were in a man's pick-up in a tunnel. The rich man was arrested for trying to kill the kids.

After the man was arrested, the boy and the girl went to Witch Mountain. They could finally go up in the purple thing from Earth to space.

Dane Fegan (8)
St Mary's Primary School, Killyleagh, Co Down

STRANGE CREATURES

One day we were moving to a new house and when we were travelling in the car, our tyre punctured and we got out. Suddenly, something jumped out of the car boot and it hit my hand. It turned round and looked at me and then it ran away. I couldn't tell Mum or Dad, they would never believe me, so I decided not to. We got the spare tyre on and off we went to the new house. When we got there, the van was already there. I wondered about that peculiar thing that jumped out of the boot. It was the size of a kitten, with pointed ears and huge, beady eyes.

I was so excited that I forgot all about the creepy thing. I went to explore the house. I ran upstairs to see my bedroom. I went to the end landing and opened a black door. I jumped back in horror. An ugly wolf was laying on the floor, it seemed to be asleep. I stumbled downstairs in fright. Dad went to investigate, but there was nothing there. He said my eyes must be playing tricks on me, but I knew he was wrong. I went to the kitchen and opened the cupboard to get a biscuit. Suddenly a slimy, hairy thing leapt out at me. I squealed as its sharp teeth bit my finger. I hit it with my hockey stick and ran to Mum and Dad. I died later in hospital.

The gremlin in the car had germs, the wolf had a disease and the beast in the kitchen spread venom on my skin.

Rebecca Kirk (8)
St Mary's Primary School, Killyleagh, Co Down

INVISIBILITY

It was a rush and excitement and then it all went wrong. You see, I made this deal with an old man, well, I thought it was an old man. He said he would give me invisibility for my soul, but I thought he meant the sole of my foot and of course, I took the deal. Here is my story, which I shall tell you as soon as I get out of the lava pool.

I thought it was great. I tripped up teachers, wrote things on the board about them and got my worst, and I mean worst, enemies in truck loads of trouble.

The man I got my invisibility from had a reddish face, black eyebrows and eyes and was very short. Do you want to know who it is? The Devil. I made a deal with him. I didn't know what to do with myself, now I am in a battle to get my life back. Oh, my life is just a mess. We all know who won, the Devil. My body, mind and soul. So I'm sending this message for someone to *help!*

Catherine Bentley (11)
St Mary's Primary School, Killyleagh, Co Down

NIGHTMARE BUS TO NOWHERE

Who was president before George Bush?

I.   Bill South
II.   Bill Clinton
III.   Bill Coach

David scratched his head. He decided to write 'Bill Coach'. Mrs Harding, his teacher, called him up at 3 o'clock.

'David, you scored the lowest in the test. Who was President before George Bush? Bill Coach. Where on earth did you get that from? I think you should re-sit the test.'

'Mrs Harding, you can't!'

'Oh yes I can!' shouted Mrs Harding.

The clock moved to four. David had been told that a bus was leaving at 4:10pm. It wasn't a normal school bus. It was bigger and very dark. The driver had large teeth, dark eyes and long hair.

'Er . . . Cornmill Av-Av-Avenue please.' The bus zoomed off. There was nobody on the bus, just the driver and David. The seats were ripped. David found the best seat and settled. It was night. The bus finally stopped, but the driver jumped off and locked the door. David looked out, he was on a cliff and the bus shook. Down at the bottom of the cliff was a lake of lava. The bus creaked, it slipped, David held on. The bus dropped down, down, down, *splash!*

The ghost of David Garfield, the nightmare of the bus.

Steven Fegan (11)
St Mary's Primary School, Killyleagh, Co Down

MATCH OF THE DAY

'Hello sports fans, I'm Andy Gray and you are here live with me on Sky Sports 1. Today we have Rangers and Celtic fighting for the Scottish Cup. Here commentating with me is John Watson. John, how do you think the match will go today?'
'Well Andy, both teams have worked really hard so far, but for me to judge who's going to win, I would probably say Celtic.'

'Well, here we go. Rangers and Celtic have come out of the tunnel. Kick-off. Larsson . . . Hartson . . . Petrov . . . Her's a corner to Celtic, Larsson is taking it. Larsson hits the ball in the air, Hartson jumps up and *scores!* Celtic have scored after twenty-seven minutes of the game. The Celtic fans are jumping with joy. Ross . . . Lovenkrands, and Lovenkrands takes it round Thompson and Petrov. What's this? Lovenkrands has *scored!* Twenty seconds after Celtic scored. There goes the whistle, see you after half-time.'

'Welcome back. Celtic and Rangers are at half-time and the score is 1-1. Here we go, and Caniggia has been brought down and has had to be taken off. Flo has been brought on. Thompson has the ball, lines it up and *scores!* 2-1. The Rangers fans are no longer smiling or singing, but the Celtic fans are. A free kick to Rangers and Ferguson is taking it. he lines it up and *scores!* 2-2. What a match! Three minutes injury time, Lovenkrands has the ball, goes towards Douglas and *scores!* 3-2 and the whistle has blown. Alex McLeish has one big, happy smile on his face and so do the Rangers fans.

Rangers are champions.'

Kirsty Coughlin (11)
St Mary's Primary School, Killyleagh, Co Down

THE CRY OF THE BANSHEE

On Friday the 13th of April 2002, I was walking home from Danielle's with Danielle, for it was a cold and dark night. People say silly things happen on this day, so Danielle and I were talking about it.

Around five minutes later, we came near to the Killyleagh Castle, when we heard a high-pitched cry followed by a loud bang. It was really scary because we thought it was the Blue Lady and we didn't know what the loud bang was. We saw a large shadow in the distance. At this time, we didn't know what it as, but when it came about five yards in front of us, we discovered it was a banshee.

Our legs were like jelly, we ran but went nowhere, our legs moving but we were not.

I wondered what the loud bang was and what the banshee wanted. It cried and cried again. It was funny, because after that cry it went away and our legs were not like jelly anymore.

Danielle and I ran down the hill. Just as we reached the bottom, we discovered a crash. In the accident three people were hurt and one was in a critical condition. Now, from this day, I know what the banshee wanted.

Ciara Nelson (11)
St Mary's Primary School, Killyleagh, Co Down

THE GHOST OF FRANK AND AARON

Jim, Mo, Jamie and Molly were on their holidays, they were staying in Killyleagh Castle. When they got there the owner, Mr Daly, was out beside the waterhole at the side of the castle. Mr Daly showed them to their rooms.

The next day, the four friends went to the haunted church. The man who owns the place, Jamie's Uncle Pat, was washing his car outside the church. They went over to him, but Jim didn't go because he didn't like Jamie's Uncle Pat. Pat showed them around his home, he showed them a room which had a table and the ghost of Frank.

'Uncle Pat, there's a ghost in that room.' Pat looked but there was nothing.

'Jamie, there's no one in there.' He showed them the rest of the house.

He took them to the old church, but he wouldn't go in, so he went back down the hill.

'Who's going to open the door?' said Molly.

'I will,' said Jamie, 'but will you all come with me?'

The door creaked open and there at the back of the room were two ghosts.

'Jim, they are going to eat you,' said Jamie. 'Why do they call one Frank?'

'They call him Frank because he was put under a spell when he was 18. Aaron got his name because he always played with iron bars.'

Frank looked down at the children and he scared them so they ran down the hill.

Jamie's Uncle Pat was not at home, but his car had blue paint on it saying, 'Help me!' they ran back to the castle and the gate was locked. Mr Daly had gone, there was a note saying, 'Help me!'

The children were scared. This meant the ghost of Frank and Aaron was behind this. The ghost had killed Uncle Pat and Mr Daly. They too had turned to ghosts.

Dean McComb (11)
St Mary's Primary School, Killyleagh, Co Down

THE GHOST THAT KILLS

One morning, Niall, Aaron, Jamie and I were walking to school and I just noticed that we were talking about the old house in the middle of the field. It was so weird, because some nights I can hear noises coming from there. Noises like *whooo-ooo* and *ooo-uuu*. So we went into class and Niall and Jamie asked me and Aaron, 'Do you want to go and check out the house?' We both agreed to go with them.

After school, the four of us started to walk across the field. The house was really old, like one hundred years old. The walls of the house were cracked and destroyed, it was really creepy and Jamie was wetting his pants by now. It was pitch-dark and you couldn't see a thing, but Niall had a torch with him. He shone it inside. We took three steps in and the ghost was sitting in a chair in the middle of the room. The ghost had a gun in his hand, and four more guns lying on the floor. We grabbed the guns and started shooting at the ghost and he started shooting at us. Suddenly, the ghost and me and Niall were falling to the ground. The ghost was dead, but Niall and I were injured.

No one knew what happened that day, except us.

Gary Morrison (11)
St Mary's Primary School, Killyleagh, Co Down

LADY GREY

This is a true story.

In a town called Lurgan a few years ago, there lived an old woman called Lady Grey. She lived in a large house with a big garden. She had a cleaning lady in two days a week and her husband did the gardening. She went to the bank once a week and then called into some of the local shops. Lady Grey was always well dressed, with all her jewellery on. She had two big diamond rings, one on each hand.

One wet winter night, Lady Grey could not find her cat. As the lightning flashed in the sky, she saw her cat stuck in the big oak tree. She got the ladder against the tree and started to climb. *Crash!* The lightning struck the tree, the cat ran away. Lady Grey was found the next morning. The doctor and then the priest were called and arrangements for her funeral began.

Her will said that she was to be buried with her family jewellery as she had no family. After the funeral, some men were whispering in the corner of a pub, saying it was a waste of good jewellery being buried with Lady Grey. After a few more drinks, they decided to dig up Lady Grey and get her rings. A couple of hours later, they pushed Lady Grey's coffin out of the ground. They cracked it open with the shovel. There lay Lady Grey with her hands folded across her chest and with all her jewellery. They snatched her necklace and pulled at her rings. The two large diamond rings would not move. They agreed to chop off her fingers. One man held her hand spread, while the other swung the shovel. *Crunch!* Off came her fingers. 'Arrghhhh!' screamed Lady Grey as she sat up in the coffin. The two men dropped everything and ran for their lives. Lady Grey went to hospital to get her fingers sewn back on and lived for another fifteen years with her cat and all her jewellery.

Orlaith Berkery (9)
St Oliver Plunkett Primary School, Belfast, Co Antrim

THE GHOST DOG

Once upon a time there was a little boy called Peter Piers. Peter was an only child. He was a very happy boy and loved his mum and dad very much. He was very excited because he was going to his Nan's to stay with her for a week while his mum and dad went to Paris.

The first night, he and his nan had a party and his nan gave him a present, it was a dog called Matey. Peter was overjoyed and let Matey sleep with him that night.

The next morning, there was a knock at the door. It was the police with devastating news. Peter's parents had been killed the day before. Peter and his nan cried and cried. Matey kept licking away Peter's tears and Peter was so glad he had him.

One month later Peter, who was now living with his nan, started his new school. He tried to make friends but the other boys in his class would not speak to him, they were bullies. They teased him, pushed him around and stole his lunch money. They mocked him by saying 'Peter Piers has big ears and his eyes are full of tears.'

That night, Peter sat in his room with Matey and cried, he missed his mum and dad so much. Matey licked his tears and he heard a voice saying, 'Please don't cry.' Peter looked around the room, then he looked at Matey and Matey said to him, 'It's me Peter, your dad. I am a ghost from the spirit world. I have come back as a dog. It happens all the time in the spirit world. Partents return as animals to protect and comfort their children.' Peter and Matey talked all night.

Matey walked Peter to school the next morning. Some boys started to tease Peter. Matey was so angry he was outside the gate and couldn't get to Peter. Matey decided to sit and wait for Peter to finish school. He heard footsteps and looked to see who was coming. It was Charlie Brodie, the leader of the bullies. Matey ran towards him and jumped up on him. He barked and then said, 'If you ever tease or hurt Peter Piers, I

will bite your nose off. I am a dog ghost and I have lots of dog friends.'
Charlie ran away crying, he never so much as looked at Peter again. He
never told his friends about Matey, but he told them never to bother
Peter again. Peter was so glad he had his dad again.

Rachel Brennan (9)
St Oliver Plunkett Primary School, Belfast, Co Antrim

A Ghost Story

Last year, I went on my holidays to a farm in Donegal. It was quite an old farm with lots of outhouses and sheds. The farm was owned by a very old farmer who used to tell us stories about things that happened many years ago. He told us lots of stories about who used to live on the farm before him, and what happened to them. He also warned us never to go near the shed at the top of the farm, as this was where the mad farmer used to live. He told us that the shed was now haunted and on certain nights, you could see the mad farmer standing at the shed looking for his family who had all run away from home because they were frightened of him.

One dark, cold night, my cousin PJ and I decided we would sneak up to the old she dot see if we could find the mad farmer. When everyone had gone to bed, PJ and I sneaked out of our rooms, grabbed some torches and headed up to the haunted shed. It was very dark and very, very scary. After about five minutes, we could see the shed at the top of the hill. Suddenly, there was a loud clap of thunder followed by a huge flash of lightning.

I looked up at the shed and saw a dark shadow of a man standing at the shed, waving his arms madly and I heard him screaming like a banshee. I looked round for PJ and he had run away, leaving me all on my own with the mad farmer! Then I felt a cold hand on my shoulder and started to scream louder than I have ever screamed in my life before. I looked round and saw that it was my daddy.
'Michael, what are you doing running around the farm in the middle of the night?' he asked.
I told my daddy all about the mad farmer. My daddy laughed and said there was no such thing as ghosts. We then went up to the haunted shed and saw that the mad farmer waving his arms was actually the shadow of a tree blowing in the wind.

The screaming was also an old stray cat that lived in the unused shed. My daddy and I laughed the whole way back to the farmhouse.

The next morning, I told everyone at breakfast what had happened and they all laughed at me, saying I was silly to believe such nonsense as the story about the mad farmer. Then I noticed PJ was not at the table and started to look for him.

PJ was never seen again. Do you think the mad farmer might have got him?

Michael Fox (9)
St Oliver Plunkett Primary School, Belfast, Co Antrim

THE WOODS

Two little girls called Nicole and Laura were on a camping holiday with their mummy and daddy. They had their own little tent. In the middle of the night, Laura thought she heard a scary owl and she moved closer to Nicole, but Nicole wasn't there! Laura crept outside and she felt a cold shiver and then she heard the owl again. As she walked through the wood, she felt something touching her feet, but it was only twigs breaking under her steps. She felt silly and went on looking for Nicole.

Then something brushed across her face - she had walked past a bush and a branch touched her face. Laura was getting colder and colder and she realised that she as lost! Then a big hand landed on her shoulder and she thought she couldn't breathe. She turned round and there was her daddy and sister Nicole.

Naimh Faloona (8)
Star Of The Sea Primary School, Belfast, Co Antrim

THE ROOM OF DOOM

It was a damp night in the Midnight Tower. The ghosts from the Room of Doom were mourning for the crystal diamond of Moria which I had stolen from them years ago. Now, people were being sacrificed to the Evorninians. So the great courage I had shown in the first Battle of the Crystals had to be called on again.

I packed my things and went to the Forest of Mirkwood, which protected the Midnight Tower. When I reached the forest, I took out my crystal and recited the protection charm, 'Ovarandinif.' I marched fearlessly up to the door of the Midnight Tower and when inside, I raced to the Cabinet of Wonders and grabbed other crystals and put them onto my Morian horse-hair bracelets. Then I came to the door of the attic which creaked open as I muttered the word 'vifa!' I stepped throught he ancient door and it gave an eerie, loud bang as it slammed shut.

I lifted up my crystals and all that was in the tower turned to dust. I picked up the ashes and suddenly everything good in the room went to Heaven, except me, since I was needed to fight yet more battles.

Caragh Cassidy (8)
Star Of The Sea Primary School, Belfast, Co Antrim

HANNAH, JAMES AND THE HAUNTED HOUSE

'But Mum . . .'

'No buts young lady, you're spending the next two weeks with your grandma Joan and your Grandpa Eddie and that's final!' James and Hannah's mum and dad were going away for two weeks and Hannah and her twin brother James had to stay at their grandparents' house.

'But Mum, their house is haunted! It's scary a-and creepy!' insisted James.

'Oh don't talk such nonsense, James! Now I've already told Hannah, that's where you're staying and that's final!'

Hannah and James felt helpless and they didn't say a world the rest of the way.

When they finally arrived at their grandparents' house, their mum and dad said their goodbyes and set off. Hannah and James heard a bang.

'Did you hear that?' whispered Hannah.

'Yeah, I think it came from the attic. Let's go up there and check it out,' James whispered back.

So they went up to the attic and to their horror, they saws the most frightening thing that they had ever seen in their whole lives. It was a ghost . . . 'Arghhhhh!' they both screamed. James was so scared that he picked up the nearest knife and killed the ghost . . . or did he?

Bronagh Bradley (9)
Star Of The Sea Primary School, Belfast, Co Antrim

A Day In The Life Of A Butterfly

I was in a chrysalis and I hung on a tree. It was hard to get out. I got out and I sat down on a leaf. The sun dried my wings and I was a butterfly at last, and I could fly. I had colours at last. I flew to a flower and drank nectar.

I can live for a month. I am a beautiful butterfly. Goodbye everyone, see you next time.

Gustav Avenstrup (8)
Towerview Primary School, Co Down

A DAY IN THE LIFE OF A DRAGON

Hi, I'm Tokao the dragon. This morning, I woke up feeling very hungry, so I went down to the town to eat some maidens. It was tough. I mean, whoever knew that they could run so fast? Finally I got them. As usual, I kept the head till last, because it is the juiciest and warmest bit of all.

After lunch, I went to see my friend the sea serpent who was blue and long. He had caught some fishermen earlier that morning and we ate them. While I was flying home, I tripped over a tree and hurt my wing and a bush caught fire, so I decided to stay there for the night. I called my friends and we sang songs. It was the best day of my life.

Conor McClenahan (8)
Towerview Primary School, Co Down

A Day In The Life Of A Schoolgirl

I woke up one morning and got out of bed. I got dressed and went downstairs. I went to school in the car. The teacher said that the Queen was coming to school. I was very excited. We did paintings of the ueen. After that, we went to do PE. When we were going back, we saw the Queen, so we all shook hands with her. She said, 'Good morning.' I didn't speak, I couldn't believe that she was in front of my eyes. Then we went to the class with the Queen. She said she was staying for the rest of the day in our classroom. That was when I got embarrassed. We were talking for so long, it was nearly break time so she let us have a playtime.

My day got even better, because the Queen came to my house for tea.

Rebekah Kirk (8)
Towerview Primary School, Co Down

A Day In The Life Of A Little Girl

One day, there was a little girl who was in the newspapers because she had the weirdest dreams that had come true. Once, she was on her way to school and when she got there she sat down and fainted. The girl's name as Rika. Rika had so much power that she couldn't control it any more. In the afternoon, she met a baby dragon that wanted to be Rika's friend, so Rika got a new friend. Rika went down to the library with the baby dragon to study, then Rika saw some evil boys wrapping up her friends by the library. Rika knew she had to use her powers to save them, and after she fainted again.

When Rika woke up, she knew that it was all a dream, but one part was real, because she still had the baby dragon.

It was nearly time for school, so Rika rushed out of the door to get to school. When she got there, she went to her classes. When school was over, Rika went with her dragon to practice. Then Rika found that she had wings, so she flew up high with her dragon, then she forgot that she was already late, so she went and flew back home.

Hazel McKinley (8)
Towerview Primary School, Co Down

A Day In The Life Of Me

When I get up, I watch TV and have some cereal. Then I walk to school and write down my homework. We did maths. After maths, we went swimming, I swam ten metres.

When we got back to school, we did English. Then we did PE and then we went home. When I got home, I played with my sister and did my homework. Then I went to bed.

Alec Dobson (7)
Towerview Primary School, Co Down

A Day In The Life Of Jehad

Once, in the far regions of deep space, an alien called Jehad lived on a small asteroid spending most of his time lying on his roof studying the stars. Before he went to bed, Jehad would look out through his telescope at the passing planets. He got very lonely and longed for company. Then one day, he noticed the asteroid had started heading straight for a blue and green planet. He ran into his house, got out his space map and found out he was heading towards the luscious, inhabited planet of Earth. Jehad made great whoops of delight!

Fifteen minutes later, he landed on a building. *Towerview Primary School, Co Down* was written on the sign outside. It was 3.30pm, he climbed in through a window and landed on what appeared to be a wooden table. A female peered over her pile of books in shock. 'What is your name?' she asked.
'Jehad,' replied the alien. 'Do you mind if I stay?'
'No, if you stay under my desk,' answered the terrified female.

Jehad was never lonely again. The female grew to love him, blaming Jehad for infecting the children if codswallop ever slipped out of their mouths.

Joshua Corry (9)
Towerview Primary School, Co Down

CHRISTMAS

On Christmas morning I woke up and I went downstairs to the kitchen to see if all the food I had left for Santa was gone. The food was gone. Then I went into the family room and there were lots of presents in the family room. I opened all the presents. I got a mobile, Tech Deck, two Harry Potter books and lots more. Then we got ready. Then my mum, dad, sister and I waited for my nanny, grandad and auntie to have our Christmas dinner. When we finished our Christmas dinner, we played on the PlayStation 2. When my nanny, grandad and auntie went home, we got ready for bed.

Nathan Morrow (9)
Towerview Primary School, Co Down

FAMILY VACATION

Homer, my dad, is a nut case, especially when he hits the dog with a frying pan. Marge is my mum. She always cooks the dinner, sometimes she burns it. My sister Lisa always plays her saxophone, my dad hates it when she plays it. Maggie is my evil little sister, she is only one this year. She is very scared of my mum when she gets angry. Bart, that's me, the soldier of the family. Once, I blew up my dad's car, he started to strangle me.

We went on a vacation and my little sister had to stay with my aunties, Zelda and Patty. They are the worst in the world. They give you dog food to eat. Poor Maggie, I'm sure she will be fine. We were flying to France, Dad's just fallen asleep, but my mum did say she was scared of aeroplanes. So we took a boat instead. It took four hours to get to France. It was fun shooting the guard in the boat.

Kristen Burgess (9)
Towerview Primary School, Co Down

A SPOOKY TALE

One day, there were two boys who had discovered a house by chance and when they entered the house, the door locked automatically. Somewhere hidden in the house, there is a key to get out. The house is owned by a magician. The boys explored around the house with spooky pictures inside a bedroom, there were faces made out of wood sticking out. The boys slept in the house and when one of the boys woke up, he noticed that the wooden faces had changed their expression.

The next morning, the boys tried to open the door, but it still wouldn't open. The boy told his friend what had happened last night and they both thought that the house was haunted. Then they heard a voice calling them. The boys were very scared, but they knew something was in there with them. When they walked up the hallway, there was a red spray paint saying, *Welcome Home Boys.* Now the boys were getting frightened.

Then the voice said, 'There is a key in this house to get out, but you will have to find it quickly, because if you don't, you will be stuck here forever!'

They knew they had to get out, so they started searching for the key. They found the key up in the attic, so they came down and opened the door and headed home.

Andrew Mailey (8)
Towerview Primary School, Co Down

A Day In The Life Of Dennis The Menace

If I was Dennis the Menace, I would show those no good softies who's boss. I would get Gnasher to make them climb a tree. First, I would like to find out why there are no tomatoes in Beano town.

'We're going to the dock,' Dennis said to Gnasher. When they got to the dock, Gnasher was going to charge at the men but Dennis stopped him. He saw that the men were strong because they could lift a crate load of tomatoes. They went to the tea hut and found old, battered mugs, just as Dennis suspected. That could only mean one thing; the softies were here.

Dennis had a plan. He got into the crane and lifted a crate full of huge tomatoes, but one fell out and landed on the softies. Dennis found out why there were no tomatoes. The softies had stopped the tomatoes getting into Beano town because Dennis and Gnasher threw tomatoes at them. Now that the problem was sorted, the Beano town had tomatoes and the people of Beano town didn't complain about Dennis and Gnasher throwing tomatoes at them.

Daniel McDade (9)
Towerview Primary School, Co Down

A GOOD TRIP

One day, my friends Hannah, Sarah, Shelly and I went on a trip to Spain. We were all eighteen. We got our passports and got on the plane, it took one hour and fifteen minutes. We were talking the whole way.

When we arrived in Spain, we got a taxi to the hotel. We had finally arrived. Heaven! The view from the window was lovely. We could see the beach and the dolphin shows. That afternoon, we went shopping. I bought a bandana, Shelly bought a robe, Sarah bought a bag and Hannah bought a straw hat.

We went back to the hotel to wash. We packed our bags and left our hotel. We got a taxi to the airport. I was sad to leave, but I missed my family too much.

Hannah Robinson (9)
Towerview Primary School, Co Down

SPIDER-MAN

There were two plumbers down in the sewer fixing a pipe. One of the plumbers said, 'I hate my job.'
'Me too,' said the other plumber.

There was a loud growl and the plumbers froze. They turned their heads and there stood a giant lizard. The lizard grabbed a plumber and took him into the darkness. The other plumber ran to tell the police about the lizard and they started the case. Peter went to work the next day and his boss said to him, 'You got good shots of Spider-Man. How about a lizard?'
'OK,' said Peters.
'Good,' said his boss. 'You will be against an opponent, his name is John, and the first person to get a photo wins £50,000, OK?'

When Peter got home, he went upstairs to his room. He lived in his granny's house. When he came down, his granny hid something and he looked. They were bills. He said to himself, 'I will win the money and pay the bills and buy a car.'

Peter went to see the professor about a giant footprint. He was not at work, so Peter went to the professor's house. The professor's wife said to him, he is not home.' Suddenly, the lizard grabbed the professor's wife and took her down into the sewer.

When Spider-Man found the lizard, he kept on saying, 'I need you to press a button so I can make the whole world turn into a lizard like me.' He was holding a device.

Spider-Man stuck his camera on the wall and stopped the lizard. The device flew on top of a drainpipe. The lizard jumped for the device, but Spider-Man grabbed the device with his web and pulled it into the water. Spider-Man was pulled in too. The lizard got hold of Spider-Man and pushed him against the button. A laser shot from the device hit the lizard and it turned him back into a man. Spider-Man rescued the man out of the water and brought the man and the professor's wife home. The next day, Peter showed his boss the photograph and he got the money!

He paid the bills and bought a red, two-seater convertible. It was all because of the help of Spider-Man, or should I say Peter?

Alexander Seawright (9)
Towerview Primary School, Co Down

THE HAUNTED HOUSE

There was once a girl called Sarah. Down her road there was an old, derelict house. It was said to be haunted. Even in sunny weather it looked really creepy.

One day, she invited her friend Jennifer to her house. Sarah called her Jenny. Once she was there, they played a while, then Jenny said, 'Let's go to that house,' pointing to the haunted house.
Sarah said, 'No.'
Jenny then said, 'You're a chicken and you're scared!'
This really agitated Sarah, so she agreed very reluctantly.

They both walked into the house. As they got in, the door slammed abruptly. The floorboards started creaking as they climbed the spooky stairs.

Suddenly a green, rotting hand came from behind a door. It grabbed Sarah by the shoulder and held her. Jenny screamed and ran.

She started trying to get out, but she couldn't find the door. The green monster said to Sarah, 'Kill your friend, or die yourself.'

In the newspaper, the headline read: 'Girl dies in old house. Friend escapes unhurt.'

Laura Allen (9)
Towerview Primary School, Co Down

THE ECHO OF VOICES

One Saturday morning, a girl called Jane and a boy called Ken wanted to go snowboarding, because they had never been before, but their mum said no all the time because they were too young to go yet.

The next morning, Ken and Jane said they were going to the city complex, but they lied. They went up to the slopes instead. They were doing fine and they loved it. They loved the cold wind in their hair and faces and the soft crackling noise underneath their feet. When they thought they were good enough, they went to the biggest slope of all, Mount Doom, where not even the birds would go. Only a few brave snowboarders would go on it.

It was a long walk up, but soon they got to the top and they both looked down. They didn't want to go, but they did. It was like a greedy hand pulling them closer and then they disappeared. They were falling down a bottomless hole. Soon, they started hearing voices and the clearest one was their mum saying, 'I told you not to go!'

Luke McClean (10)
Towerview Primary School, Co Down

TALE OF THE MESS MONSTER

One dark stormy night there was a young boy called Jake who was writing a ghost story for school. His teacher, Mrs Ferguson, gave him extra homework for putting a whoopee cushion under Jamie's reading cushion.

He had two ideas for his story. He could go to his sister's room and call it the 'Tale of the Mess Monster' or go to the graveyard and call it 'Zombies' Return'. He decided to do the first idea, so he crept into his sister's room and saw her under her bed muttering something. He thought she said, 'Stupid Mum, making me tidy my room.'
Jake thought he could bribe her, so he said, 'I won't tell Mum, if you let me in.'
His sister turned around and she was eating what looked like a crisp packet and her face was dirty - very odd. After a minute, she was pulling him into another world. It looked like the dump. It smelt like the dump. It was the dump! He got up and saw a giant rat which seemed to be talking. It was saying, 'You've done well,' and it turned to Jake and said, 'kill him!' More rats came out of the ground. Jake grabbed some air freshener (which he was lying on) and then he woke up.

He was lying on the floor with air freshener in his hand and with his head in the bin in his sister's room. He ran to his sister and said, 'Get . . .' He dropped dead to the floor. His sister was laughing, and she was never seen again.

Joshua Walker (10)
Towerview Primary School, Co Down

DEEP IN THE WOODS

Deep in the woods there was a little girl. She had roamed the woods since she was twelve years old. Here is the story of what happened.

This little girl was called Aliesha. She was sleeping over at her friend's birthday party, they were going in the woods. She wasn't scared at all, despite all the stories she had heard, she was in fact really excited.

She left the house at six o'clock and started walking to her friend's house. In case you don't know, her friend's name is Lisa. When she opened the gate, to her surprise, Lisa jumped out from the bushes and scared the wits out of her.

Lisa's dad drove them into the woods and set up the tent by the lake. They cooked their tea over the fire, got ready to go to bed. They got into the tent, into their sleeping bags and zipped the tent up. Just then, the fire went out. Lisa refused to move until Aliesha got more firewood. Aliesha agreed and went out. Fifteen minutes later, Lisa heard a really loud scream coming from the forest. She jumped up and shouted at the top of her voice, *'Aliesha!'*

She ran home as fast as she could. Her dad came running up and asked what was wrong. She was out of breath, but told him quickly. They rushed as quickly as they could, but found nothing.

In the morning, the police came round to investigate. They found nothing either. People still say they can hear her screaming at night.

Natalie Fisher (10)
Towerview Primary School, Co Down

A Day In The Life Of Bart

My name is Bart Simpson. I like football and I hate school. My hobbies are skateboarding and playing with the dog. When I go to school, I make a fool of myself and I made a T-shirt, it said, 'Down With Homework.'

I hate my sister Lisa, and so do my friends Nelson and Milhouse. She tries to stop me doing bad things. My little sister Maggie and my mum are very annoying. My dad is a pain. All he does is drink Duff Beer and eat doughnuts. Did I mention he is fat and hairy? Maggie was sick all over me and my mum is worse at times. At the end of the day, after tea, I go to bed.

Lee Glenfield (9)
Towerview Primary School, Co Down

A DAY IN THE LIFE OF KING ZOVA

King Zova is a fat, royal king who doesn't do anything except eat food. He's been eating all his life.

'Five McDonald's a day, three KFC's and three Burger Kings at night. That's my daily schedule, and you can't delete my daily Big Mac, said King Zova.

'Sorry King Zova, but you have to cut down on your food,' explained his servant Aneta.

Queen Zeta entered the room. Queen Zeta is a tall, skinny lady with long blonde, curly hair. She is quite annoyed.

'Where's my crown, idiot!' she screamed. She snatched the crown and left.

'You should go on a diet, or you will explode!' said Aneta.

A big knock interrupted them, it was Lorna, the information lady.

'Your wife has been kidnapped, she has just gone to Las Vegas!' she said.

He demanded that Aneta get his private jet. He took everyone he knew with him. As they arrived, King Zova didn't feel well. He fell flat on the ground.

'It must be the McDonald's he ate earlier,' said Aneta. He soon got lifted by a crane. They found Queen Zeta in a secret hideout. King Zova didn't feel well. He thought he was going to explode in 3, 2, 1, *Boom!* But nothing happened. King Zova didn't explode.

After a few years, he was a regular sized king. Everyone was happy!

Laura Salmon (9)
Towerview Primary School, Co Down

THE CLUMSY CROC

One day in the zoo, there was a crocodile called Clumsy Croc. He was called that because he kept tripping other animals up, like Clucksy Hen and Hiss, the snake. Every morning, Clumsy Croc would get up then go for a bath in the river. It would wake up Hiss in the tree. After his bath, he would shake his tail up and down. While he was doing that, all the water would end up on Clucksy Hen and in her food. Everyone would complain, but Clumsy Croc would just not listen to Clucksy Hen or Hiss.

But one day, Clucksy Hen said, 'I can't take any more of this. I am putting a stop to this once and for all.' Clucksy Hen said to Clumsy Croc, 'Come with me, Hiss the snake wants to talk to you.'
They said, 'Clumsy Croc, why can't you *stop* banging your tail up and down, soaking us and making it go into Clucksy Hen's food? And can you please not stand on my tail?' said Hiss.
Then Clumsy Croc ran off in tears and said, 'Why don't they like me?'

One day, Clucksy Hen and Hiss were in trouble and they screamed, *'Help! Help!'* Clumsy Croc came to the rescue. Clumsy Croc laid in the river, then Clucksy Hen and Hiss walked over his back, but he tripped and Clucksy Hen and Hiss fell into the river. But just in time, Clumsy Croc lifted them out by the tail. They said, 'Three cheers for Clumsy Croc!'

He was not called Clumsy Croc anymore, he was called Super Croc because he had saved them from the river. That was how life went on, but he still kept tripping Clucksy Hen and Hiss up. They still liked him.

Jonathan Maguire (9)
Towerview Primary School, Co Down

THE HAUNTED HOUSE

One day there was a little boy called Joshua. He swore he wasn't scared of ghosts, so his friend Mark said he would give him five pounds if he went into the haunted house and came back out again, alive. So Joshua walked up the path, past the graveyard and up the stairs to the door.

When he got inside, the first thing Joshua saw was a big, spiral staircase. He stepped on the first stair and it fell. Right where he was standing fell. When he hit the ground, he heard a thump, thump, thump. He called out, 'Who's th . . .' He couldn't finish his sentence because a big wisp of smoke went down his throat, then he fell to the floor.

Some time later, he woke up. The room was lit by two red beams coming from where the doorway was. He felt something hairy crawling over him. When his eyes got used to the dark, he found out those little hairy things were spiders, thousands and millions of spiders crawling over him.

He ran for the door but was blocked by something like sticky rope. He knew what it was straight away, it was a giant spider's web. He heard a big snip, snip of the giant spider's pincers. He felt the rope-like web wrap around him. After five minutes, his legs were completely covered with web. In a few more minutes, he felt the last draw of breath come out of his mouth. Joshua died and Mark felt like killing himself for making Joshua go into the haunted house.

Mark Cooper (9)
Towerview Primary School, Co Down

A NIGHT AT MY AUNT'S

My mum told me I had to say at my aunt's house while she went away on business. 'Get your bag ready, because you're going straight after tea.'
When I heard that, I nearly screamed the house down. My aunt's house is haunted, I'm sure about that. She makes me sleep in the top bedroom of the house. So I ran up the stairs in a fit. 'OK, calm down now,' said Mum.

I started to pack my bag, making sure I had a torch and spare batteries just in case. I packed a lot of clothes, because at the top of the house, not much heat gets up. I packed my teddy and an extra blanket. So I cam downstairs and had my tea. I kept on thinking, this will probably be my last meal.

I zipped up my bag and brought it downstairs. I put my bag in the car and I got ready to go. My mum said I was a very good girl to go, so she would buy me a bag of sweets to share with my aunt, and a drink. So I got in the car and ate some sweets. I thought they would be good hidden in my bag, in case someone or something ate them. When I got there, my aunt welcomed me with a cup of hot water and a cookie. I went in the front room and had my snack. I was tired, so I said goodbye to my mum and went up to my bedroom.

It was freezing. A sudden coldness shot down my spine. My aunt told me to go to bed and she would wake me up in the morning for breakfast.

Then the adventure began. I went downstairs early to explore. I found a door that I had never seen before. It was very dusty. I opened it. It made a loud creak, I hoped it hadn't woken my aunt. I walked in, it led to a staircase. I carefully held on and walked down it. At the bottom, I saw a very bright light. I wondered what it could be? I walked on a bit more, ready to run if something came. There were two entrances, so I went down the first. Something flew over my head. I did not run, because it was only a bat. I ran into something at the bottom. I saw the light getting brighter. When I tried to run, I found something was caught round my feet. I managed to get out. Once I got out, I looked back. I told my aunt. She said it was her garage, it hadn't been cleaned out for years. She said I shouldn't have gone down there.

Rachael Carson (10)
Towerview Primary School, Co Down

THE CREEPY MASK

There was once a little boy called Jimmy. He and his brother went to the local Hallowe'en store to get some party stuff. They both saw a very scary mask. Jimmy bought it and took it home.

The next day, it was his party day. He started to set up the banners and scary things for his party. When everyone came, he went away to put on his mask.

When he came back, he could not keep control of it. He was eating everything and chasing everyone. He managed to get it off in time, before he hurt anyone.

The police came over to his house and said, 'What happened here?'
'It is the mask,' he explained.
The police went and said to themselves, 'What a pile of nonsense!'

Jimmy threw the mask out and never heard of it again.

Richard Kennedy (10)
Towerview Primary School, Co Down

THE RETURN OF THE SHADOWS

It was a perfectly normal English summer, or so everybody thought. Sally Tarkeen was thirteen at the time. She had two sisters and a brother, but they don't come into the story.

It was 11.15pm when the cries of 'Night Mum, night Dad,' rang through the house. Sally was last to go to bed. She fell asleep almost immediately, but at 00:00am, she woke up. What was that rustling sound? 'It sounds like a cloak dragging through leaves!' said Sally to herself. 'There's no one in here but me!' Little did she know, there were The Shadows!

The next night, she woke up at exactly the same time. This time someone was speaking to her, he said, 'Sally, Salleeee.'
Sally whispered, 'Who are you? What do you want?'
'We are The Shadows, we want your *soul!*' said the eerie voice.
Sally screamed, 'Go away, leave me alone!'
The next thing she knew, she was being smothered - by what? Shadows. It all went black.

The headlines next day read: '13-Year-Old Sally Tarkeen Found Dead In her Bed.'

Jessica Warke (10)
Towerview Primary School, Co Down

THE BUTTERFLY

Once upon a time, there was a butterfly. He laid tiny yellow eggs and caterpillars came out. He flew all around. During winter, he would fly west. His wings started to break up, but suddenly they came together. Somehow he carried his tiny caterpillars. He found a plant pot and the babies made a cocoon, but suddenly when they came out, there were spiders, moths, tadpoles, centipedes and millipedes everywhere.

What a nightmare!

Chris Walton (8)
Towerview Primary School, Co Down

SHARK

One day, Sharky the shark was playing with his friends, then his mum called, 'Sharky, dinner's ready.' Sharky zoomed home like a rocket, but something was wrong. Sharky was not moving, and then he foundhimself trapped in a whale's mouth. Sharky looked around, then a big, enormous flood of water came in and the shark could not breathe. Then a big, big *blast* of water shot up from under Sharky and then Sharky found he was free and everything was calm. Sharky started to swim home, then the whale came back and swallowed Sharky in one mouthful and he was digested!

Sharky was never seen again!

Benn Laird (8)
Towerview Primary School, Co Down

SCHOOL

I was in school having a spelling test like yesterday. I ran out to play in the playground. The minute I walked out of the door, I realised I wasn't in school. 'I'm on the moon!' I yelled. 'I think I am. Look, there are craters, it must be the moon!' I was floating up and up, away from the moon. I landed on Earth, but I didn't know where I was. I saw a man and I asked him where I was. He said something I didn't understand, I thought I was in China. The man directed me to the airport where I caught the next plane home.

Glenn Wylie (8)
Towerview Primary School, Co Down

A Day In The Life Of A Butterfly

It was a nice, sunny day when the butterfly woke up and went to get nectar out of the daffodils. He flew over to another garden, where he met other butterflies. The butterflies all decided to get together for a beautiful butterfly dance. They rose high in the sky and the sun shone off their bright, colourful wings.

As the evening got colder, they found shelter in a great big green cabbage.

Connor McGibbon (8)
Towerview Primary School, Co Down